THE JUDGE: PART I

BY

IAN R B MORRIS

PROLOGUE

They had become Mr and Mrs Philip Carr with the sweep of the forger's pen. Their precious lives obliterated, snuffed out, as if they had never existed. They were now new people with no past and a future they had yet to build.

He had left the hospital early under the cover of darkness. He could not afford to stay there. The wound had not quite healed and although he was bound up tightly with bandages, it occasionally ached, reminding him how fortuitous he had been. Looking over at his new wife as she snuggled asleep next to him under an airline blanket, a pillow puffed-up under her head, he knew another reason why he was blessed. They had arranged the marriage in a hurry. She had bought tickets for Grenada and booked the hotel that morning under an assumed name. It had been ridiculously easy to procure the fake passports they were using. She had drawn every penny she had from her savings account as soon as her bank had opened. Fifty thousand pounds. Not much, considering how long they might have to survive on it. £5,000 had been eaten up buying the passports. £10,359 including taxes on the flights and they had yet to sort out accommodation. They'd have to hope they found a buyer for their treasure quickly but then, given the contents, it seemed unlikely they'd be too reliant on the remaining cash for long.

As he looked across at her asleep in her seat, she looked impossibly small and impossibly beautiful buried under her blanket, almost child-like. He wanted to pick her up in his arms and shield her from everything. He knew it was ridiculous, that she was a very tough customer who would not thank him for trying to cotton ball her. She was gorgeous and he admired her jet-black silky hair, tousled about her delicately Asian face. He loved her almond-shaped brown eyes and her lightly tanned skin. Since getting on the flight she had been rather zealous in her consumption of champagne and had quickly fallen into a deep slumber. He also felt light-headed and marvelled at the haze of delirious intoxication that was peculiar to the over-indulgence of champagne.

He had never flown first-class, and had he not been so preoccupied he would have marvelled at the unprecedented space that his long legs enjoyed. Inspite of his slight inebriation he resisted the fatigue that pulled at his eyelids. He would only sleep when he had to, when he was forced to.

Watching her chest rise and fall he felt privileged. She could have had anyone she wanted but she had chosen to spend the rest of her life with him. He had almost lost her. Fear of what might have been gnawed uncomfortably at the pit of his stomach. To the outside world she had not been changed by what had happened. She was still self-assured on the surface. He knew otherwise. It was he who had to comfort her when she woke with her screams from unimaginable dreams, drenched from head to foot in sweat. He had tried to talk to her, but she was not ready. He knew what had happened to her physically, the police had told him that, but what no one could tell him was the mental state she might be in. The truth could take years to surface.

Flying to Grenada with a one-hour stopover in Bridgeport, Barbados, they would spend two nights at the Moorings Hotel before sailing back to St Lucia on a ninety-foot, fully crewed yacht, stopping at all the islands on the way. This was what they could laughably call their honeymoon. The honeymoon was really nothing more than an elaborate cover. They would never make it back to St Lucia on the boat if everything went according to plan.

He was with the only woman who mattered to him, apart from his daughter. The events that had thrown them together had also inextricably altered the lives of many other people. He regretted that he had not had more chance to explain. All he had managed was a quick phone call to warn them.

He had no doubt that they were being scrutinised now. He had already looked around the first-class cabin at all his fellow passengers. He dared not look too closely, his own neuroses telling him that if he did more than the odd furtive peek suspicions would be aroused. But he had selected a couple of candidates in the front row of the economy section. There was something about them that gave them away. They were two men in their late thirties, early forties. They looked uncomfortable with each other. They did not smile or chat with the amenable hostess. They stared ahead of them with a steely, determined look in their eyes.

He had taken a look at his suspects when he had used the toilets in the economy section. The first-class toilets had been engaged. They did not look at him at all. Something was not right about them. The severity and firmness of their features seemed to suggest a killer's icy core. The cut of their grey suits seemed wrong, they looked like they'd be more at home in combats.

Sitting in his seat he began to feel weary. He glanced at her, Helen as she was now known. Would the name ever seem right, would it ever suit her? Or, would it always serve as a reminder of the fact they were no longer themselves?

He was a fugitive, albeit a willing one with a beautiful wife and an uncertain future. They were fugitives. He had never voiced his opinion to her. How could he, she had been through so much already. She had given up everything she had for him. She could have walked away. He knew that their chances of success were slim. They would never allow them to get away. There was too much at stake. Sleep overcame him. A fitful sleep in which he dreamed of memories and of the dangers yet to come.

ONE

It was a normal night, he was late, and she'd done most of the bottle of claret before he arrived at El Vino's, the local to all those in the legal profession.

Peter rushed in.
"Good evening. Sorry I'm late, I got tied up doing a bloody affidavit for a punter who came in off the street. For the pittance we get they expect a damn silver-plated service."
She was pleased to see him and enjoyed the kiss he gave her on the lips as he bent down to greet her. She loved the taste of cigarettes on his mouth. Without saying a word, he flopped down in the chair opposite her and poured himself a healthy glass of claret. Lighting up a cigarette, he took a deep drag.

"How has your day been? If it's been half as lousy as mine, I do not want to know. Don't tell me; the bloody Roland case? I've had it up to here with that one. You said not to tell you but I'm going to anyway."
He smiled at her. She liked his rebelliousness at times and wanted the opportunity to have a good moan herself.
"That bastard Mather only went and chewed my arse up this afternoon about our handling of the case. Seems he is some sort of chum with Hodge, they're probably in the same lodge together. They both lunch at the RAC. Anyway, I got the usual diatribe and veiled threats. They presumably suck each other's knobs when they get the chance."
"Peter, you are dreadful."
"I know. That's why you love me," he said grinning

inanely at her. Leaning across the table he touched her lightly on the hand. Peter was not a demonstrative or tactile man and she took great comfort from these little gestures of mutual affection.

"What are we going to do tonight? I fancy a curry takeaway and an early night."

Peter downed his glass and poured himself another. Stubbing out his cigarette in the ashtray on the table, he quickly lit another. It just seemed right that he should smoke. She had a mental blank when she tried to picture him without the obligatory cigarette attached to his bottom lip.

"First let's finish the bottle, seems a shame to waste it."

Peter looked down at his pager and was about to switch it off when it rang. If he had turned it off a few moments earlier, he would not have known who was calling. The shrill noise ruptured her romantic reverie.

"Oh Christ Peter, couldn't you have left that damn thing at the office for once?"

Peter had volunteered for duty solicitor at Holborn Police Station some years ago. Not because he enjoyed being disturbed at all hours of the day and night, they both hated that, but because it provided him with a never-ending supply of criminal clients and useful connections with the local constabulary. He rotated his services with other solicitors. Peter quipped it may just be a drunk, he could be home by 3am!

Getting up from the table he began to head for the telephone near the bar. Turning back towards her he winked. "Let's go do justice." She laughed at his catchphrase. He as ever had used his charm and dissolved any irritation she felt.

Peter was as unhappy as Naomi that the pager had chosen another awkward moment, but he enjoyed the role he played as a duty solicitor. He knew that nine times out of ten he would be called to defend someone who had been in a fight or driven home after one too many. Occasionally he was lucky and hit the jackpot. Some of his best clients had been obtained in the early hours of the morning at Holborn Police Station. This was his way of paying back his debt to society and helped to appease his conscience when he became disillusioned with the rich and well-connected clients that he normally dealt with.
Tonight however, he did not feel particularly saintly, and the choice between a cosy lustful night in bed with Naomi or a cold miserable night down the police station did not appear to be a difficult one. Reaching the phone in a quiet corner of the bar, he picked up and dialled the number of the station.

"Holborn Police Station."
"Hello. This is Peter Ritchie the duty solicitor. I've got a message on my pager to call Sergeant Jarvis. Is he the custody officer tonight?"
"I'll transfer you."
"Thank you."
The line went silent for a few seconds as the desk officer transferred the call. Sergeant Jarvis asked Peter whether Bobby Black, a male prostitute, was one of his clients. He knew Bobby quite well and had acted for him on a number of occasions for soliciting charges. He liked Bobby, a runaway turned prostitute. A prostitute that had turned

out to be anything other than that which he had expected. Every couple of years he got himself into trouble.

He had forgotten the details and the conversations they had had, but like many of his clients he expected him to turn up like a bad penny every few years or so. If it was a simple charge for soliciting he could be home in an hour or so to enjoy his promised romantic tryst with Naomi. He was beginning to think that the evening was picking up.

"It's a bit more complicated than that Mr Ritchie," The sergeant began as if reading his thoughts. "He's dead."
"Sorry, did you say dead?" Peter queried.
"Yes. He was found in his flat early this afternoon. He died in somewhat mysterious circumstances."
Peter felt agitated. He could not see what the hell this had to do with him. He felt sorry for Bobby but if he was dead he did not see what he could possibly do for his ex-client. He was not a heartless man, but that was a fact.
"Sergeant. I fail to see what this has to do with me."
"I'm coming to that sir. If you could just be patient," the sergeant said tersely. "He was found dead this afternoon and we found your name amongst some of his papers and we know you represented him on a number of occasions. He had no living relatives that we know and we were wondering if you could identify the body. I appreciate that this is a little unorthodox but we have to be sure it is him."

Peter was shocked. He was moved that Bobby had

no traceable living relatives, not even one, and shivered with the isolation and loneliness that he must have felt. To die alone with no one but a solicitor with whom you had nothing more than the most fleeting contact to identify your earthly remains.

"Of course. What do want me to do?"

"If you could come immediately. DCI Brown, who is leading the investigation, will meet you at the morgue at St Bartholomew's Hospital."

"I'll be there in twenty minutes."

Placing the phone down slowly his own mortality flashed before him and made everything seem trivial. He, unlike Bobby, would never die alone. Walking silently back to table he noticed that Naomi was looking at him.

"What is it Peter? What's the matter," she said full of concern.

"One of my clients, a prostitute, is dead. I've got to go to the morgue and identify his body."

He tried to sound matter of fact; he did not want to show his true feelings.

"I'll be home as soon as I can."

"That's alright. I've got an advice to write anyway and a bloody mode of trial to prepare for tomorrow."

He was not listening to her as he turned and left the bar hurriedly. He had to do the right thing for Bobby Black.

TWO

Peter Ritchie stood in the refrigerator room of the morgue. It was known amongst mortuary employees as the refrigerator because that is what it was. What else could they call a room that had one wall full of double-decker gurneys hidden behind two cold thick metal walls? He felt the cold seeping out from behind the doors and shivered as it crept into the marrow of his bones.

Nothing had been done to disguise the purpose of the room and the cold fluorescent light added a clinical brightness, devoid of feeling. He could understand why funeral parlours insisted on disguising their true function with homely fixtures, fittings and furniture.

The whole room reeked of antiseptic, the cold metal surfaces shining. Looking at the thick metal doors before him he tried to imagine what it would be like to be behind them. The thought spooked him and he pictured in his mind's eye all those cold, dead, staring eyes following him around. Which one was Bobby being kept in? Drawn into some sort of game he moved his eyes from door to door, trying to decide. Strange chemical smells hung about in the air and wafted under his nose from the nearby autopsy suite, masking what he could only describe as the lingering fetor of death.

All thoughts of romance had been pushed firmly to the recesses of his mind when he had arrived at the mortuary to meet DCI Brown. It had taken Peter ten minutes to get to the hospital by taxi. A cold drizzly night, he had stared musing out of the window the whole way. The taxi driver had tried to make pleasant conversation with him but he barely heard a word the man said and simply grunted vague approval. The driver eventually took the hint and lapsed into silence.

Arriving at the hospital he made his way to meet DCI Brown at reception, they had exchanged a few initial pleasantries. He had never met him before. He had met a large number of policemen throughout his career but could not claim to know any well. Policemen were by their very nature suspicious of lawyers, seeing them all in the same sceptical light. They were the enemy as much as the criminal. Without them their lives would be infinitely less complicated.

Brown had, initially, appeared to be pleasant enough. Brown had led them both to a deserted office down the corridor. Flicking on the fluorescent tube light, Brown had sat down at a table and, pulling out a battered packet of Silk Cut, offered one to him. Peter saw the smoking sign on the wall clearly another rule that everyone just ignored.
"No thanks. I'll stick to my own."
Peter did not want any bond to form between them. He had no intention of forming any friendship with this officer. Pulling out his packet of Benson and Hedges he lit his own from the lighter Brown proffered before him. They had both sat in silence for a few moments, savouring the first few drags of their cigarettes. Smoke floated around them in lazy spirals towards the light on the ceiling. Peter was unnerved by the complete silence within the building. In fact he was not happy at being in a hospital at all. He found them strange, alien, uncomfortable places cloaked in

death, decay and disease. As soon as he stepped over the threshold of one a peculiar feeling always overcame him. Swamping his senses, ramming home with certainty his own tenuous mortality.

"Before you identify the body I would like to thank you Mr Ritchie for coming down here under these extraordinary circumstances."
"That's alright. I'm glad to be of any help that I can for a client. Even an ex-client."
Peter still could not believe that Bobby was dead. He had only seen a dead body once before. His grandfather, a cantankerous old man who had seemed ancient to him at the tender age of seven. He had not liked it when the old man had moved into his parents' house. He had felt like his space had been invaded by a mean-spirited man. Peter had been happy to leave him behind when he went to school, not for him the love and fondness for an eccentric old man. He had died quite suddenly, three years after his arrival, in the middle of the night one dull, cold, grey Saturday evening. His absence not being noticed until twelve the following day, a Sunday, as his mother had prepared the traditional roast.

Seeing him lying in the bed, white as a sheet, with his teeth settled at the bottom of a glass of strident on the bedside table, his eyes wide open, the distinct smell of stale defecation hanging in the air, did nothing to help him grieve. It had been the root cause of a recurring nightmare that had haunted him for years; that still woke him up screaming in the middle of the night every now and then. It had not been the body, not the staring eyes, not the smell of stale urine and shit. It had been the teeth. All perfect and white with pink plastic gums, floating innocently in the glass. No one had thought to tell him that when you grow old you sometimes lose your teeth. And for years he had believed that your teeth fell out moments before you expired. A scary thought for any child.

Peter had not thought about this for years. He knew it was irrational but he could not help himself. If Bobby had no teeth, Peter would not be able to control himself.

"Of course as I am sure you understand, in every death we have to have the body formally identified before we can carry out an autopsy. Even if the deceased is known to us. Unfortunately, you will have to identify the body in the morgue itself, they don't have a formal identification suite available here at this time of night," Brown said officially.

Peter was pulled from his reverie as he replied "Yes, the sergeant who telephoned me said as much. What I cannot accept is that I am the only person apart from the police who can identify him. What about friends, family? There must be someone."

Brown smiled at him. "Mr Ritchie, Bobby was a prostitute. All his friends would have been prostitutes, pimps or drug pushers. He mixed with the lowest kind of scum, who all close ranks when something like this happens. As for family, Bobby, if that was his real name, which I doubt, was probably a teenage runaway who had not seen his family in years. If they knew where he was they didn't lift a hand to help him. Just because he is dead it doesn't mean they change."

Peter was beginning to remember the conversations he had had with Bobby over the years. The detail would come back to haunt him later. What Brown was saying did not ring true. He did not blame Brown for being hard-nosed about things. He was, after all, only being realistic.

"He was murdered then?"

"Well, forensics are still at the scene, but we're not looking for anyone else."

Peter felt himself getting angry. Realism was one thing but a complete lack of interest was another. "What do you mean you're not looking for anyone else? He was murdered wasn't he? - Scum like him usually die like this."

Peter did not understand. "Die like what? Do I understand that because of who and what he was you do not intend to investigate the matter fully?" he snapped.

"Mr Ritchie. You can take it from me that this case will be accorded the priority that it deserves." Brown was clearly becoming angry as well. He did not appreciate being called out after hours to wet-nurse a solicitor.

"Mr Brown. We are both professionals. You can take it that whatever we discuss is strictly between us."

Brown took a deep breath. "You don't need to know how or why it happened. All we want you to do is to identify the body. The investigation has nothing to do with you. You are not acting in your official capacity as the deceased's solicitor. In fact you are not here in any official capacity at all...."

"Exactly my point!" Peter interrupted.

"Any help you can give us will be looked upon

favourably," Brown responded.

Peter was not going to put up with this. Rage and anger were beginning to boil to the surface. "I would like to remind you that I am volunteering to do this. I do not have to. Either you co-operate with me and tell me everything or I get up and leave right now. It's no skin off my nose. Everyone, even 'scum' like Bobby deserves the full protection of the law. If he was murdered you have an obligation to investigate and bring his killer to justice. I also do not like your attempts at coercing me into helping you," he said through gritted teeth.

"I am doing no such thing. I am merely pointing out that your help will be noted in the future." Peter was not going to be blackmailed by anyone. "In other words I do as I'm told. Right! Well it's not alright and I do not think that your superior officer would be pleased to hear about it." Brown could barely disguise his contempt for Peter as his lips peeled back from his face in a snarl. The mask had slipped. Peter was seeing the true being hidden behind the carefully polished visage.

"You fucking solicitors are all the same. You sit in moral judgement with your sanctimonious heads up your arse while the police drown in bureaucracy, spending cuts and growing crime figures. Instead of helping the police you hinder us at every opportunity. You preach to us about justice. Who is it that gets scum like that off the streets? Who protects you when you sleep in your bed at night? You waltz into stations armed with the law and free guilty people to re-offend. It is my business to see that priority is given to certain cases. Who cares that one more prostitute has been killed? Tell me, who cares Mr Ritchie?"

Peter was shocked by this tirade of abuse and anger. He watched Brown in silence for a few moments. He flicked his cigarette angrily into a Styrofoam cup that was conveniently sitting in the middle of the table.
"Mr Brown. I do not want to argue with you over what you believe to be the role of the solicitor within society. You may have abandoned all hope for the system of justice in this country but I have not. Call me principled, call me naïve, call me whatever you like. But do not insult my intelligence. Now you can tell me exactly what you know or I will leave."

Peter could not help thinking that Brown was hiding something, if it had been a straightforward murder why had he exploded?
"I will tell you what I do know if it will get you off my back, but I don't want to hear that you have been interfering with the investigation of the case in any way. Do I make myself clear?"
"Perfectly."
"Since you know Bobby's history better than I do I will not detail that. From what we have worked out so far it appears that he died at about three o' clock today. The coroner who attended the scene ascertained that Bobby died during a sex act that went wrong. Until the autopsy tomorrow morning he will not be able to tell us the precise cause of death, but he could tell us that some form of asphyxiation took place. In short, he probably took a trick back to his flat who wanted something kinky, Bobby did as he was asked and it all went horribly wrong. Simple really." Brown

talked quickly with little feeling. "Doesn't it make you sick what these perverts get up to? How could anyone get a kick out of throttling themselves at the point of orgasm?"

Peter could not understand it either. His curiosity was aroused. "You said that he was probably with a trick when this happened. How do you know that?" Peter asked.

"Well without spelling it out. His hands were tied behind his back at the point of orgasm."

"So what?"

"Mr Ritchie, unless our Bobby was an exceptional person, someone had to bring him to a state of heightened pleasure. If you get my drift?" Brown made a suggestive hand movement in the air, he continued. "Also unless he was a contortionist he couldn't have tied his own hands behind his back."

"Could someone have strangled him during this act?"

"Yes. Maybe if someone tightened the cords around his neck. But there was no sign of forced entry and whoever was there made sure that no obvious trace of his existence was left behind, so unless forensics come up with something we will probably never know what actually happened."

"What if he was murdered?" Peter asked.

"Forensics are still checking the scene, nothing incriminating so far. If you want my honest opinion, it was an accident pure and simple".

"But your sergeant said that he died in suspicious circumstances."

Brown pulled a grimace that parodied a smile. "Did he? Well I certainly did not authorise him to say anything of the kind and I repeat we are not looking for anyone else. I think I have answered everything that you need to know. Can you identify the body?"

Peter knew that he could get no further information from Brown. He asked to see the body alone. He had developed an intense disliking of Brown during their conversation. He did not want to meet him again for a very long time but somehow he suspected that he would.

Standing in the refrigerator Peter was suddenly disturbed by the mortuary assistant. He nearly jumped out of his skin with fright.
"Did I scare you sir?"
"No. Not at all."
He was scared. The young assistant looked like someone who would be at home on the set of the Night of the Living Dead. He could tell that he was going to be one of those people who chatted endlessly. He opened the heavy door and pulled it back. Reaching for the lower gurney he began to slide it out. Peter heard the scrape of metal against metal. He could not see much as the assistant stood in the way.
"Some people say to me, 'Bowers, how can you do the graveyard shift?' They say it spooks them. Personally I've never been a daytime person. I prefer the night. Gives me a chance to study up on my anatomy. Don't you think so sir?"
He had finished pulling the gurney out. Peter could not keep his eyes off it. He could see Bobby's body inside the body bag. It looked hard, unreal, unmoving.
"Sir?"
Peter forced himself to reply "Oh sorry. Yes I quite agree."
He did not want to think about the assistant. He

was spooked enough as it was. After his discussion with Brown he didn't know what to expect. Was he going to be sick? Brown had said that Bobby had been killed sometime today. Therefore he concluded that the body had been found today. How bad could a body that was less than a day old look?

"Ready sir. If you just step forward so you can see better."
Taking two deep breaths, Peter stepped forward. His knees were beginning to buckle under him. Straightening them with force of will he stepped closer, still smiling at the assistant. Trying to look as if he did this sort of thing all the time. All he could see in his mind's eye was his grandfather's false teeth in the glass. The assistant appeared to realise his unease.
"First time?"
"Yes," Peter replied.
"Don't worry. This one isn't too bad. Saw him when they brought him in earlier. Had a quick look at him myself. I'm studying to be a doctor. Third-year med school. Only work a couple of nights a week otherwise I'd never attend classes, this is pretty easy work really."
The assistant leaned into the body bag and, taking hold of the thick industrial zip, began to pull it back. In the sterile silence of the room the sound tunnelled its way into Peter's brain. The material undid like the jaws of a crocodile, exposing the body beneath. Watching as the zipper made its way downward he first saw Bobby's shoulder-length blond hair, then the top of his forehead. Peter had expected his skin to look pale and marble-like and although it had faded a little it still had that all-year-round

suntan. Next the zipper exposed his finely chiselled nose and eyes. The piercing blue eyes were open and bulging in their sockets. They seemed to be staring straight at him. Finally he could see his mouth and throat area. He had expected the worst. Apart from severe bruising around the throat and a blue tinge to the skin around the mouth, he looked no different.

His memory was suddenly jolted into place. Even in death he had maintained that androgynous quality that had made him so popular in life.

The first time they met was three years ago. Peter remembered because it had been his first week as duty solicitor at Holborn station. It was also his first year at Martin Mather & Co. It had seemed nothing out of the ordinary at the time. The station had called him at three in the afternoon to represent a teenage prostitute who had been brought in for possession of cocaine.

He did not like drug offences, or drug offenders for that matter. It usually involved a sad individual. He derived no satisfaction from representing someone who was bombed out of their mind. As if the drug involvement was not enough, his soon to be client was also a male prostitute. A man forced to sell himself to feed his need. He could not imagine what depths of despair he would have to travel to before he would trade himself for a fleeting physical and mental stimulation. It made him question his desire to be a duty solicitor.

Peter attended at Holborn and was shown into Bobby's cell for an interview. The officer shut the door behind him and locked it. Peter always felt claustrophobic in the cells. They were so small and uncontaminated that the walls seemed to close in on you. The bars on the tiny frosted glass windows, if you were lucky enough to have windows, only bore down on your subconscious more.

He had once been hauled to the police station during his student days for drunk and disorderly behaviour. They kept him in a cell all night and let him go the next day without charging him. He had claimed that it was the police state's attempts to clamp down on the creative and political will of the radicals within the student community. His brief stay in the cells was, he thought, the biggest hindrance to the life of crime in his existence, even though he became somewhat of a celebrity around the campus.

What he did not tell his fellow students was that it was scary, tedious and dull and, at the end of the day, rather humiliating. The police had played everything by the book with bored complacency and a little irritation at having to deal with a minor drinking offence. He had not committed any crime and they knew it, they had simply reacted to his ill-timed, smug, slurred statement that he was a lawyer, as if this would warrant him some form of immunity. Of course they probably would have let him go if he had not uttered those deadly four words.

Having been told the offence he was surprised to see that Bobby was a young, good-looking, smartly dressed man. His blond hair was scraped back into a long ponytail at the back. Bobby looked up at him as he walked in. His piercing blue eyes were clear and intelligent. He stood up and walked towards him, extending his hand. They shook hands. Peter noticed the flash of an Armani label on the right breast hand pocket of his designer shirt as they shook. A neatly pressed blue denim shirt. A clean smart pair of black jeans. Peter had envisioned someone with greasy hair, dirty clothes and dull, unfocused, bloodshot eyes. Bobby moved with panther-like grace, his body honed to perfection by relentless physical exercise.

He smiled as they shook hands, exposing perfectly white Hollywood teeth. This must be some mistake, Peter thought. They must have shown me to the wrong cell. This man was not the type he was used to dealing with. He was about to say as much when Bobby spoke.

"Hi. I'm Bobby. Mr Ritchie isn't it?" he spoke confidently, with a neutral London accent. "Yes." He did not know what else to say. He was thrown off balance momentarily. Everything he had intended to say was forgotten.

Bobby moved back to the bench seat along the far wall and casually sat back down with one leg on the bench and the other off. He was still smiling. He was relaxed. Too relaxed for someone who had never been held by the police. He had been in this situation many times before.

"Come and sit down. I guess you want to interview me." He indicated to the blue legal pad underneath Peter's arm. "That is what you're here for, right?"

He was mocking him.

Peter regained his poise and sat next to him on the bench. A whiff of expensive aftershave skimmed under his nose. Opening his legal pad and taking out his gold plated cross ballpoint pen, he turned to Bobby. He did not think the interview would take long. "Right Bobby if I can deal with the formalities first...."

Bobby interrupted him. "I can't say I'm a pro at this Mr Ritchie but I have been here before. My name is Bobby Black, I was born on 19th August 1980 and I live at 2 Brewer Street, Soho, London, which I own. I live there with a friend of mine. I am currently unemployed for the record. Off the record I am a prostitute. I have been cautioned for soliciting three times in my career but so far have avoided a criminal record. Apart from that I have a clean bill of health so to speak. Call it the luck of the gods. Call it influence, call it what you like."

Peter was annoyed that he had taken charge of the interview and he struggled to scribble down everything he said. He was annoyed but he also began to find himself warming to the character. Only twenty-one years of age, he seemed years older, wise beyond his years.

"That," Bobby continued, "is the boring bits dealt with; anything else you want to know?"

Peter was intrigued. "Well before we move onto the offence itself I think we ought to flesh out your background a little more. What about your family, just in case we need someone to stand bail or to be a surety?"

Bobby thought for a moment. "Listen, before we get into that, what's your first name? I've told you mine. I can't keep calling you Mr Ritchie can I?"

Peter did not like where the conversation was going. Certain clients, only certain established and lucrative clients, called him by his first name.

But since he probably would not see Bobby again it could do no harm.

"Peter. Now about your family."

"Peter. I don't have any family or at least none that I could or would care to call on for help. The truth of the matter is I don't even know where they are anymore. I left home at thirteen years of age to seek fame and fortune in London. My mother was an uncaring whore, all she needed to know was where she could get her next fuck and bottle of vodka, only difference was she did not take money for pleasure." He paused. "My stepfather, well her then current lover, and father of my youngest brother was a sadistic bastard who believed the key to discipline was torture. She had six children by different men. When I left I did them both a favour. They've never tried to look for me or me for them. Do I fit the profile that you had in mind," he continued without sentiment or emotion.

Peter was building up a mental picture of the childhood he must have suffered. A poor uneducated family living from hand to mouth just to survive in a council house somewhere in London that probably should have been torn down years ago. Compelled to run away, Bobby was forced to live on the streets where some pervert coerced him into selling his body in order to survive. It made him aware of the advantages he had been given by his parents. But he was being skilfully sidetracked from the issue at hand. He had to be back at the office before five. Looking at his watch he saw that it was already three-fifteen. He would not get away before four now.

"Well Bobby, interested as I am in your

background, the fact that you were brought up in abject poverty will do you few favours in this instance, particularly in view of your current occupation." He tried to take control of the conversation.

Bobby smiled again, once more exposing the expensive dental work. "Did I say I was brought up in poverty? People like you Peter are too willing to blame a person's financial circumstances for the path they assume in life. As a matter of fact my mother was a relatively wealthy woman. We lived in comfort in a large house in Dulwich. My brothers and I attended a private pre-prep school. I had the same and better social advantages than many of my contemporaries. I chose to abandon them, not them me."

He was playing games with him. He did not seem to be at all worried about his predicament. Peter did not have time for philosophy.

"Bobby, while I find this very interesting I don't really have time for this. Don't you realise that you are in a lot of trouble? Can we get back to the issue..."

Bobby laughed, a throaty infectious laugh full of kindness, and interrupted him again. "Peter, I was found with a couple of lines of coke on me. I'm not a dealer, they know that. It was purely for recreational purposes, for the punters. Hardly a hanging offence. I never use it. I have to keep my wits about me in this game. If it gets to court, it's my first offence, I'll get a slap on the wrists, a large fine and a record. So what?"

Peter was annoyed that he could be so glib. Peter had to stamp some authority on the conversation.

Bobby was running rings around him. Peter was used to being intellectually superior to his clients. Here he was being made to look like a moron. The problem was that Bobby was probably right about his analysis of the case. Clients normally turned to him for advice. He did not expect them to know the letter of the law and yet Bobby had succinctly summed-up the position.

"So what. If you were so sure, why do you need me? It may not be as straightforward as that anyway. The courts take drugs offences very seriously. This is not something that you can shrug off. If you breeze into court with this cocky attitude they're likely to lock you away and throw away the key. If the prosecution brings up the fact that you are a known prostitute, the court is not likely to treat you like an ordinary member of society. Now I could not care less whether you want my help or not, just say so now and I will go. I am sure that neither of us want to be here, we both have better things to do."

He often used the shock tactic with clients who refused to see sense. It usually shut them up if he threw the worst-case scenario at them. It also helped in the event that the judge handed out a more lenient sentence. It made him look an even better lawyer and made the client feel he had been brilliantly represented. Looking at Bobby's amused face he knew it had not worked.

Bobby laughed again. He was smiling again. Bobby clapped his hands in joy.

"That all depends on whether it ever gets to court. As I've said already, I don't think it will."

Peter could not believe his naiveté. "What exactly do you mean? Do you think for a minute that the

Crown Prosecution are going to overlook a possession of class A drugs by a local prostitute? You have been charged already. The police are not going to just pat you on the back and send you out the back door saying that it has all been a terrible mistake and tear up the paperwork."

He was still smiling. "Believe me it will not get to court. Certain members of the bench wouldn't be able to maintain their impartiality. What I haven't told you is that the police only stopped and searched me because they wanted me to blag on someone else. It's their way of levering other information out of me."

Peter could not believe what he was hearing. He knew that the police did things like this. But it would have to be pretty sensitive or valuable information for them to set up someone. What could a prostitute amongst thousands possibly know that was so special?

"Am I right in thinking that they set you up? Because if that is what you are saying I'll come down on them like a tonne of bricks. You'll be out of here within hours."
Bobby explained "I'm not saying that I didn't have the stuff on me. They're too clever for that. They knew that I'd bought it. They had stitched up my supplier with some trumped-up charge or another. He was to tell them next time I bought any in exchange for the charges being dropped."
Peter was incredulous. "You still have a case for entrapment. Anyway what could you possibly know that they want?"
"You would be very surprised. Let me put it this way. The police wanted to teach me a lesson."

If he was as cocky as this with the police he was not surprised that they wanted to teach him a lesson. He laughed out loud. He was beginning to think that Bobby suffered from some mental disorder.

"Talk me through this one Bobby. Humour someone who has worked in criminal law for a number of years. If they wanted to teach you a lesson surely all they had to do was arrest you for prostitution? They would not have to create an elaborate and dangerous, ruse to net you. Why would they?"

Calmly Bobby replied, "You see Peter, there you go making assumptions again. You're assuming that I'm just any old prostitute wandering the streets of London hopping in and out of punters' cars for a quick tenner here and there. As prostitutes go, I'm pretty much queen of the castle."

Peter could not help but smile and even though he tried to suppress it, he could not. It was corny but in the circumstances it was funny.

"You see Peter some of my punters are very important people. I mean very, very important people. They give me a certain degree of protection. They couldn't do much if I killed someone or something like that, but your average bust for prostitution or living on immoral earnings, that sort of thing, they can have it sown up within hours. All I have to do is make a call."

Peter was confused. "What the hell are you still here for then. Why haven't you made this mysterious call yet?"

If he was making it all up he would have to come

up with something pretty clever.

"They won't let me. Simple as that."

The case against the police was getting stronger by the minute. It was so far-fetched it had to be true. Despite his better instincts Peter found himself believing this man.

"If that is true, Bobby, and I'm beginning to believe that it is, then they have fundamentally breached the Police and Criminal Evidence Act. Anyone being held in detention is entitled to make one phone call."

Bobby was patient, "You still don't get it, do you? This is all part of the game. You don't imagine that this is the first time I have been hauled in over the years. They know that if I'm allowed to make that call they won't see me for dust and the smell of shit falling on them. They are trying to make me sweat."

Bobby unquestionably knew what he was talking about. Hard as it was for Peter to believe him.

"Where do I come into all this then?"

"I'm afraid you're a pawn in my attempt to checkmate them."

"How?"

Peter was beginning to feel helpless. There was obviously nothing he could do for his new client. He was intrigued to find out more.

"Well by asking for the duty solicitor I've shown them that I'm not falling for it. If they don't let me go you can kick up a stink until they do. They'll have to give in. You'll make it clear that I've told you everything. They can't risk any of this coming out. Can they?" Very clever indeed, Peter thought. He was right. The police would have to let him go.

"You appear to have thought of everything. But what if your protection as you call it was removed for whatever reason. What would happen then?" Bobby was short "That's simple, I'd be killed." He said this as if he was ordering a pizza or asking a favour from a friend. Peter would not be so blasé in the face of eventual death. If he was lying he was the most convincing liar that Peter had met.

Peter reasoned with his client, "surely if it came down to it you could bargain with the information you have?"
"It doesn't work like that Peter. Think about it. If I trade the info the people I work for couldn't allow it to happen. Believe me when I tell you that there are people who would try their best to see that I never made it. People at the highest level. Then there are those who want the info desperately for that reason. If my protection failed and I gave them everything they wanted, do you think they could protect me? Either way I die."

Suddenly Bowers the mortuary assistant brought him out of his reverie. He was standing in front of him looking at him strangely.
"Are you alright sir, do you want to sit down? Was he a friend?"
Peter looked at the assistant. The assistant busied himself zipping up the body bag and returned Bobby to his chilly frozen temporary resting place. It dawned on him that he had been drifting along in his little world without a care for anyone else. It was not difficult for a solicitor to do. Like many professionals you had to become casehardened in order to survive the pressure, both physically and emotionally. Every now and again it paid to

remind yourself of certain cases that moved you. He had always treated Bobby as just another client, another statistic.

"No. But he was my client."

The assistant had intimated that if he ever needed any information on current cases all he had to do was get hold of him. He would be present at the autopsy as part of his anatomy revision. He had called in a favour from the chief pathologist. He would not get much sleep, but it was worth it. Hands-on experience was how he had phrased it. Peter had taken down his number and exchanged it for one of his business cards. Still in a state of shock, he had paid little attention to what Bowers had said, keeping his responses to nods of the head. He left soon after.

THREE

Naomi had worried about Peter all evening. She had tried to settle down to her case for the morning but she couldn't concentrate for long.

Finishing her glass of wine at El Vino's she had set off for home immediately. Walking back to Temple underground station on the District and Circle lines she had sat quietly on the next available tube to Barons Court, the nearest stop to her flat. From Barons Court it was a short five-minute walk to her cosy, basement flat in Glazbury Road. She always took the same route. She enjoyed the fresh air after a long day cooped up in court and office buildings. It was however, not a long enough walk to endanger her low level of fitness. She might enjoy the crisp air as it filtered through her lungs and cleared the fogginess of tiredness that was clouding her brain, but she did not want to sweat.
She knew that she was lucky. She never had to diet or exercise in order to maintain her near-perfect figure and it had altered little since she had left school at eighteen. She was aware that most of her female friends and colleagues were insanely jealous of this biological factor. They regularly accused her of being anorexic, bulimic, neurotic and riddled with various other diseases and neuroses, in order to deflect their own ability to pile on the pounds. She knew that she could be flippant about it. With this in mind she resolved to telephone the Balti Curry House on the Hammersmith Road for a delivery, once she got home.
Shopping was not her strong point either. She knew that the fridge contained an out of date

packet of Marks & Spencer salad, fresh linguini Verdi and a tub of not-so-youthful mushroom sauce. Peter always complained that there was never any food, but never made any effort to buy any himself. They therefore lived on takeaway and restaurant meals. Peter had mistakenly believed that when they had first got together that she, as an Indian woman, would be a superb cook who would serve him his favourite curry dishes without complaint. That had been his first big mistake.

Like many second-generation Indian women the only thing that differentiated her from her English friends, who juggled a career as well as everyday life, was the colour of her skin. She had quickly proved to Peter that she had difficulty boiling water, let alone making Bombay potatoes.

It was a cold night and she watched her breath as she padded along the pavements with the sound of traffic reverberating in her eardrums. When she had first moved to London it had taken her a long time to get used to the constant noise involved in living in a thriving metropolis. There was nowhere you could go to escape it. For a few months it bothered her enormously, preventing her from sleeping, and she often had to escape at weekends to the relative quiet of her parents' home in Weybridge. After a while she found that she no longer noticed the noise.
She arrived at her home, a large Victorian building, split into flats. Carefully negotiating the steps down to her flat she let herself in. The steps were a real problem and, she vowed, as she had a thousand times before, to get something done about them. They were verging on the dangerous

in the winter because they were so steep and narrow. No accidents had occurred, as yet, but she expected Peter to fall down them any time when his large feet slipped. The wrought handrail down one side was her gesture towards safety. She had had it installed soon after she took possession on her twenty-first birthday, the result of an extremely beneficent gift from her parents.

She loved the flat from the day she moved in. It was unusual for a basement flat because instead of being dreary, dark and damp, it was bright and homely largely due to the stylish designer interior that had been commissioned by the previous owner.

Like most flats in London it was not large, but with one double bedroom, a bathroom, an ample galley kitchen and a huge, open plan living room and dining room it was bigger than most. The room that really sold the place had been the garden room on the back. With double doors opening onto the garden and a glass ceiling and windows in every outside wall it had looked perfect even when she had viewed the property in the winter. Light streamed into the room all through the year and she had quickly turned it into a dining room.

The garden was a lush green, low maintenance, paradise with vines and creepers smothering the walls, fronds and palm-like plants erupting from the ground at every opportunity, threatening to encroach on the flat itself. A large pond was sunk into the floor of the upper terrace. It was like her own secret garden buried within the heart of London. It had been the perfect base for her when she was at bar school and in pupillage. Once she had become a tenant at her present chambers it also proved useful because as a junior barrister she had spent many hours in the West Kensington County Court which was conveniently located a few minutes' walk away on the North End Road.

Dropping her bag in the entrance hall she put on the lights as she moved through the flat. She did not like the dark. She even insisted on sleeping with a light on in the hall, much to Peter's annoyance. This was part of her routine. She always checked the whole flat before she settled down for the evening. She knew that if anyone had broken in she could do little to repel them, it simply made her feel better, more secure, and she certainly could not contemplate any work before this was done. She had lived alone for a long time. Since Peter had lived with her he had offered to carry out the ritual. She had to do it, that was the whole point and she could not make him understand this, try as she might.

Having checked the whole flat to her satisfaction, she phoned the Balti House for her takeaway. Standing in the hall waiting for the Balti House to pick up, she looked around her living room. The whole thing was tastefully done even if she thought so herself. It was chic and elegant without being flashy or ostentatious and reeked of the Conran shop. She ordered the same as always. Chicken tikka masala, naan bread and onion bhaji. She did not particularly like hot spicy foods, preferring instead the westernised mildness of an English Indian takeaway.

"Just because I'm Indian does not mean I have to like Indian food does it?" She was constantly amazed at the racial stereotype blinkers that even the most liberal-minded people insisted upon wearing. Even Peter who verged on extreme socialism had questioned her. Socialism had become, she believed, inextricably linked with political correctness. It was right on for people of any ethnic background to once more embrace the fabric of the culture that they had once been forced by colonialism to abandon. She had no intention of espousing her own culture, which was as alien to her as it was to those who wanted her to. What did they know anyway?

She had decided not to order anything for Peter. It had sounded like he was in for a long evening and she knew he would not be hungry after something so traumatic. She knew the signs, his mouth had been grim and his forehead tight.

She remembered a conversation they had had a year ago. He had returned home looking pretty austere and pale. He of course pretended that nothing was wrong, blaming his quiet demeanour upon a headache. It enraged her that men never opened themselves up to anyone and she had to coax the details out of him. No matter how close she felt to him there was always something between them. He had been given the task of looking after another solicitor's caseload while he was away. Peter was happy to do it, although he knew nothing about the subject having long ago forgotten the basics learned at law school, because he owed him a few favours. Fending off most of the clients, he only had one appointment arranged for the week. The mother and beneficiary was coming in to sign the oath for administrators because her son had died in testate.

Her son had been one of the victims of a gay serial killer in London. She lived in the West Country and would only travel to London on that day. She could not or would not rearrange the appointment. The appointment had gone well until she broke down in tears when he had tried to take her to a neighbouring firm of solicitors to swear the oath. It had deeply affected Peter. All he could do was take this pitifully shrivelled old lady into his arms in the middle of a busy street. She had seen tears in his eyes when he told her. He, of course, had tried to blame it on a slight cold that he was developing.

The food arrived about half an hour later. She felt like kicking herself. Instead of getting on with work she had sat down to enjoy early evening television. It was amazing how interesting television became when she had work to do. Sitting curled up on the large sofa in the living room, she had eaten from the foil trays, washing it all down with a glass of red wine. Peter would have moaned at her for being such a slob, but he was not here to complain.

Every now and then she would catch sight of her bag, abandoned in the hall. Ignoring it for as long as she could, by nine o'clock guilt forced her to turn off the television and get on with her work. Looking at the prosecution bundle and the advice to counsel neatly folded and tied in white and pink ribbons respectively, she did not know which

one to deal with first. She was making excuses.
She had to deal with both and would be up half
the night. She was suddenly fatigued. Not being
able to decide she settled on reading both
instructions to see which involved the most effort.
As she already knew, the prosecution bundle
proved to be the hardest or at least the most
complicated.

The facts of the matrimonial brief were quite
straightforward. Mrs Howard the petitioner was a
new client from one of her instructing solicitors.
She noticed with satisfaction that this was a
private client. That meant she would make a hefty
billing even if the advice was all she was required
to do. Skimming the facts it was obvious that the
marriage had irretrievably broken down and that
the ground for divorce was unreasonable
behaviour. Nothing obvious, just a number of
incidents and events over a number of years by
the husband that added up to unreasonable
behaviour. Taken separately they were almost
laughable. The most important factor was how the
petitioner reacted to them. For instance, during
the ten years of their marriage the respondent had
refused to give her any housekeeping whatsoever,
even after the birth of their two children. He
refused to show her or the children any affection
and treated them all as slaves. He even insisted
on sleeping in a separate room. He never took her
out and although he was not violent he
systematically wore her down with petty put-
downs and assaulted her verbally as a mother,
wife and woman.

The instructing solicitor had listed a number of
specific events. Naomi was not at all surprised

that the woman had ultimately had a complete nervous breakdown. She would have cracked under considerably less pressure. She wondered what made men like the respondent tick. He had everything. Money, a beautiful house, wife and children, and yet he had to destroy it all. This was going to be a messy fight. He had made this woman's life hell for ten years but he would stop at nothing to prevent her getting anything.

Naomi had seen it all before. If she was retained as counsel no doubt she would be overseeing an expensive and futile fight over an insignificant and invaluable piece of furniture at some stage in the proceedings. In one case she had seen a couple forced to go to mediation over a kitchen chair. In the end the case cost them both so much that the chair was just about the only thing they had left. She remembered her client's face the day she had told her that she had been awarded the chair. It had been a portrait of victory.
With this cautionary tale at the forefront of her mind she drafted her advice to her instructing solicitors. She always did these in longhand. It would be typed up in chambers. Finishing the advice and reading through her prosecution bundle and making pertinent notes took less time than she had anticipated. Looking at her watch she saw that it was half-past eleven. Peter should have been back by now, she thought to herself.

A pin-prick of fear pierced her soul, leaving a lingering thought that something had happened. She knew this was ridiculous. As duty solicitor he was always working weird hours. Sometimes they hardly saw each other and more than once the subject of giving it up had been broached. She did not really expect him to give it up. After all she would not thank him if he asked her to give up her work.

I'll be damned if I'm going to mope around here like a lovesick puppy waiting for its master to come home, she thought to herself. Putting the kettle on in the galley kitchen she made herself a cup of camomile tea. She switched the television back on and tried to make herself look as relaxed as possible in case he returned. As Newsnight blared she slipped off to sleep.

She awoke later. Someone was prodding her gently in her left arm. She was dreaming about the mode of trial tomorrow. She was being chastised by the judge for turning up in his court wearing no clothes.
"Yes, Your Honour I'm sorry, but I was up half the night, I overslept and somehow my clothes just did not seem important," she mumbled.
To her the dream was real and she was beside herself with embarrassment and shame as the entire court admired her nudity. They were all laughing, laughing at her.

Dragged back into reality, her eyes opened. Peter was leaning down looking into her face and shaking her arm.
"Hello darling. You were dreaming. It's twelve, I've just got in. Time for bed."
She did not have time to think about much. He had woken her up. She was angry with him. Very angry, as she always was when anyone woke her. The noise from the television punctured the nerve centre of her brain like shards of broken glass.

"For Christ's sake Peter, why the hell did you bloody wake me? You could have left me here and covered me or something."

She really hated him momentarily.

"If I hadn't, you would have complained at me tomorrow about your bad back and neck," he said gently. "At least you didn't kick me like last time," he continued.

She drew herself irritably up the sofa to a sitting position. She knew he was right but with the mood she was in she could not admit it. Feeling herself coming round she felt less groggy and muddled. She was sure there was something she had to ask him.

"As I always say, denial is acceptance." He paused.

He was smiling but she could see something glinting in the corner of his eye. Something recondite and sad.

"Silence is acceptance...". She continued one of her favourite phrases. "Acceptance is double acceptance."

"Now let's get to bed," he continued.

Her sense of humour was finally returning. "Yes, we were going to have an early night?"

His face slipped, the smile cracking.

She had never seen him so desolate. He turned his back to her. He had been to the morgue to identify one of his clients. How could she have been so stupid? So insensitive. So selfish. She instantly regretted her earlier burst of anger.

"Shit Peter. I'd completely forgotten. I'm so sorry." She really did mean it.

Quietly he replied "that's all right. It's been a long evening."

She knew that it was not okay. Getting up from the sofa, facing him, she placed her hand on his right shoulder.

"Do you want to talk about it?"

He kissed her lightly on the nose. She could smell his breath on her face. He had been smoking like a chimney again. She also detected the faint odour of alcohol. More than likely vodka. He had a tendency to drink this if he needed to get drunk quickly without detection. He did not look drunk, but never did. His capacity was mythological. This was not the time to mention it however and whenever she brought his health up they had a blazing row. The moaning could wait until morning. She returned his kiss lightly on the cheek.

"I tell you what," he said smiling weakly. "I'll tell you all about it when we're in bed. All I can say for now is that something just isn't right about it all. I don't know what yet, but I'm determined to get to the bottom of it."

As he spoke a late night news summary began on the television as he finished speaking. They both watched it silently. The third story mentioned Bobby's death. The newscaster did not mention Bobby by name, stating that the death was a tragic accident. The police were appealing for any witnesses to come forward. Finally he stressed that the police were not looking for anyone else in connection with the incident. They showed Bobby's picture. An old fuzzy photo that looked at least five years old. Peter hesitated his glance on the television momentarily. Naomi knew somehow that this was the man that Peter had been called upon to identify.

Peter turned off the television and quietly led

Naomi to the bedroom. She had no idea what he was going to tell her.

FOUR

Sir Justin Gordon Hodge, High Court criminal judge, opened his eyes, as usual, at 7.45am. For an instant his eyes refused to recognise the surroundings as he shook off the last vestiges of sleep. For a fleeting second his heart was filled with a surge of panic. Sleep had momentarily removed the faculties that dictated who he was. As his eyes and memory refocused, he remembered.

He was seventy-five years old. He felt every bit his age as he stretched his complaining limbs surveying his room with detached familiarity. The old four-poster bed he was lying in, the mahogany tallboy beside his bed and the French antique dressing table. His silk dressing gown was hanging on the back of the door. His clothes from the night before were neatly folded on the Chippendale chair that propped open the door to his dressing room and en suite. He knew them all like the old friends they were. He had always liked this room. It was a pity that he did not get the chance to sleep in it often. He was in his bedroom in his wife's home.

He drew back the heavy red velvet curtains from the large Georgian casement windows, allowing dawn to fill the room. Looking out at daylight spreading across the acres of well-manicured gardens like a golden quilt he enjoyed the peace and quiet. This was his favourite time of day. The advancing years had quietly pilfered the need for hours of endless sleep. He preferred the still calm before humanity truly woke up and laid claim to its domain.

Opening the lock on the top of the window he slid the window open. The frame had been in place since 1788 and he marvelled at how well it had stood the test of time. Only the twentieth-century paint gave in to the ravages of hardy English weather. Noting the flaking paint he reminded himself that he would have to get them painted again. He didn't know if it was his age, but he could swear that the times between painting them grew less and less. That's what is wrong with this country, he thought to himself, no one has any pride in what they do anymore. Loss of pride was in his opinion the first step down the slippery spiral to anarchy and chaos. Despite what people thought of him, and there were many who detested him, he loved his country.

He watched the gardener from his vantage point as he began to rake up some leaves that had fallen onto the long gravel driveway, meandering down to the imposing gates that signalled the end of his property. The gardener was in his staple uniform, checked shirt, loose at the collar, an old threadbare three-piece herringbone tweed suit that was clearly too big for him hung loosely around his frame. On his feet he had a pair of old walking shoes with the tops of the trouser legs tucked into them and on the top of his forest of dark hair sat a cloth cap. As he watched the man at work he tried to remember the man's name. He thought it was Mr Geoffreys - but then again he couldn't say for certain. He did his job well. He could not remember the gardens looking better. Geoffreys was new and he approved of the transformation that had taken place.

He had made a point of never interfering with how his wife ran the house, but he had wondered why the previous gardener had been sacked unceremoniously. He did not interfere, choosing instead to keep an eye on things from a distance. He was pleased with the results in the garden. As the gardener stooped to pick up the leaves and dropped them into a wheelbarrow, he could have sworn he recognised someone he hoped never to see again. Something familiar in the gait. He froze for a moment, transfixed by an unimaginable terror. But that was impossible. It could not be. He knew the fate of that particular individual.

Dismissing this thought as absolutely idiotic he turned and walked to the full-length gilt mirror that adorned the far wall of the bedroom. The mirror had been a family heirloom and was the only thing he had wanted to keep when his mother had died. Looking in the mirror, he was six feet tall with a shock of white hair, fairly lean for a man of his age and position and dressed in handmade silk red and white pyjamas from Gieves and Hawk. He even looked good in pyjamas, he thought to himself. He admired his face for a few minutes, deciding that he looked at least twenty years younger.

His silver hair added to the image and made his tanned skin look all the more healthy. With a sense of satisfaction he noted that there was hardly a line. He caressed his face fondly remembering all the lines that should adorn his visage. This was, of course, thanks to the highly secret facelift that he had undergone some years ago, but since no one had discovered this fact he had always put his youthfulness down to healthy living. Vanity, he thought to himself, was not the preoccupation of film stars alone and he was after all in the public eye. Image was all-important. Or was it something else? The need to obliterate any family resemblance?

For a moment the figure in the mirror reminded him of his father and his heart was filled with fear and self-loathing. He shut out the tide of memory before it could sweep over him. He had almost been transported back to his parents' vicarage in Bramley, Guildford. The only time he was powerless to blank out his mind was when he slept, another reason why he did not sleep well.

It was the cruellest of blows that he should be so like his father. They could have been brothers. If he had not died naturally the judge would have killed him. Even now he was still trying to kill the spectre that haunted his every waking hour.

He smoothed down the pyjamas, his good humour evaporated by the icy fingers of recollection, and headed to the bathroom, following his reflection in the mirror as he did so. He turned on the ornate gold taps of the Victorian bath. The whole room filed quickly with steam from the hot water, causing a film of moisture to condense on the mirrored walls around the bathroom. He was thankful that he could not see his reflection clearly.

He had reason to be in a bad mood. He remembered and relished for a moment the terror he would incite in many people throughout the day. Not only had last week's trial run over, but what had seemed to him to be a simple prosecution under the Protection of Children Act 1978 for the possession of indecent photographs and had been listed for three days had run into the full week due to the defence counsel's insistence on dragging out the whole affair by calling witness after witness that did little or nothing to advance the case any further. He had lost his patience with the case on Thursday and had decided that the defendant was guilty.

By Thursday afternoon he had turned his attention to other matters and asked counsel for the defence exactly what they hoped to achieve by their needless time wasting. He had reminded her that the court's time and resources were not to be played with. That they were not hers to waste. This usually struck a note with the jury, who did not want their precious time wasted either and was his standard method of getting them to see things his way. He had given her his best withering look. Miss Naomi Brahman was either stupid or very brave because she gave the standard barrister-with-no-defence reply that all witnesses built up a picture of the defendant's character. He knew that she was attempting to give the monster a human face, a side which the jury could identify within themselves.

He felt some compassion for her. He had rarely, if ever, come across a more hopeless case. She had been valiant in her attempts to create something out of nothing. He knew that they all knew he was guilty and if they didn't yet they would by the end of the trial, he'd see to that. She should have kept it short, just convincing enough to fool her client into believing he had received his money's worth. What he hated more than anything was wasting time on a hopeless cause. He had tried to help her out, to bring the matter to a speedy conclusion.

Ignoring him, she insisted on battling on. He had made his view distinct. She should have taken note of the signs and cut her losses there and then.

Crossing swords with the judge was not a positive career move and he had tried relentlessly over the next two days to destroy her case. Miss Brahman and her instructing solicitor Peter Ritchie from Martin Mather & Co had appeared before him on a number of occasions before. He did not like Peter Ritchie. He was arrogant and confident. Much like he himself had been many years before. He almost admired him for that but what he could not admire was Ritchie's slovenly preparation of cases, his messy, unkempt appearance, his ability to disregard authority and his adoption of a wing and a prayer policy for each case he worked on. But what infuriated him most was that he was in fact a good lawyer who could, with application, become one of the best. Thus he liked to dent Ritchie's law of averages.

Ritchie's senior partner Martin Mather was an acquaintance of his from his club and he had taken the chance over a lunch the previous week to outline all of Ritchie's failings. He had, he believed, beaten Miss Brahman and convinced the jury that the defendant was guilty. If he had not done so already, he would certainly make sure his message was clear in his summing-up today. He would have to be careful however. If he did not make the facts and the law very clear to them she would definitely appeal. The prospect of which would shatter his untainted record as a High Court judge sitting at the Old Bailey. He was certainly going to enjoy himself today. As he undressed and climbed into the steaming full bath, he began to whistle tunelessly to himself, his previous fears instantly forgotten.

FIVE

In the cold light of day Peter had time to think
about the events that took place the night before,
until he got to the office at any rate. Having said
goodbye to Naomi, he left for the office at seven-
thirty. This was unheard of but he needed to
think, and he had mountains of work to get
through not least of which the R.V. Roland case.

As a case in point, R.V. Roland was a simple case
of defending a child pornographer at the Old
Bailey. The client was legally aided and so he had
given Naomi Brahman, friend, lover and trusted
counsel in such cases, the usual instruction to
drag out the trial for as long as possible in order
to bump up the legal aid bill. There was, of
course, little or no defence to the charge as Mr
Roland had been under surveillance for some time
by the 'Porn Squad', who had arrested him while
he was taking an indecent photograph of an
eleven-year-old in his living room while his wife
was at her pottery class.

As if this was not bad enough, Mr Roland had a
loft full of child pornography in both film and
photographic form that he had been selling and
distributing to fellow child pornographers
throughout the country and all over Europe. He
even had a catchphrase or jingle for the service he
provided, 'Porn R Us'. Mr Roland had therefore,
whether wittingly or unwittingly, covered all the
offences under Section 1 of the Protection of
Children Act 1978 and the Director of Public
Prosecutions had presumably been only too
pleased to give her consent to the institution of
proceedings. If only all such cases could be so cut

and dried, she must have gleefully thought at the time.

The lack of defence had not worried Peter as he had a reputation for taking indefensible cases and at least achieving the lesser sentence available, and occasionally winning. He tried not to think about the offence, even though it sickened him. He had to see it as just another case.

He had no doubt that Mr Roland would be found guilty by the jury and at the start of the trial the previous week he had been hopeful of a suspended sentence for a year for a first-time offence and a large fine. This had however been eroded as the week had progressed. The judge, Sir Justin Hodge, or Hitler as he was more fondly known within the hallowed corridors of the Old Bailey, had made it increasingly clear that he had grown impatient with the line of defence and had systematically attacked and undermined it to the point that he would have every justification in throwing the book at Mr Roland and imprisoning for the maximum of three years.

The judge had made the defence look so incompetent with his constant references to both counsel and Martin Mather & Co's abilities to handle the case that Mr Roland had begun to complain about their services by the end of Friday's hearing. This had culminated in one of Mr Roland's relatives complaining to the colonel late on Friday evening. Peter had therefore lost his enthusiasm for the case and had ordered a trainee solicitor to sit behind Naomi today for the summing-up of the case. If Roland had no faith in his abilities, let the filthy pervert rot in jail, as he deserved.

Peter made a mental note to improve the calibre of his clients in future and moved his thoughts on to more pressing and urgent matters, he needed to get organised and get to work. He leaned across and kissed Naomi before heading into the kitchen to make the first of many coffees for the day.

Naomi had woken up enough to remind him that they had an impending lunch date with her mother on Sunday. She always referred to her parents' home as the temple. The house was nothing like a temple, in fact it was a comfortable modern mansion in St George's Hill, Weybridge, the heart of the richest seam of the commuter belt. The temple was more in deference to her parents' strict Hindu beliefs than the house's architecture. Which gave nothing away about the owners' religion or race.

Peter enjoyed the lunches, he loved their food, even if it was hotter than any Indian food he had ever had in a restaurant, and found her parents' antics hilarious.
"If I wasn't there to witness it myself I would say that it was impossible for anyone to act the way they do in the twentieth century."
"Slight change from usual," she said. "Father's not going to be there, he's gone to Kashmir to sort out some of our land."
Peter did not know much about where her father's money came from, she did not like to talk about it if she could help it. She was not comfortable with her family's wealth, painfully aware that their vast fortune had been made on the backs of the poor.

All he knew was that they had fled the principality of Jammu and Kashmir in 1962 when the Chinese invaded it in response to a previous Pakistan offensive. Her father had never gone back except to reclaim vast tracts of land that he had owned prior to the invasions.

Peter pulled himself together, he needed to concentrate on the matter in hand. He left the house. He was not normally early to work. It was, therefore, as much a surprise to him as it was to the staff when he arrived at 7.45am although, to be precise, only the receptionist and a couple of the secretarial staff had arrived. He presumed also that Hale was also within the confines of the building. A man whose domain was both the heaven of the accounts department and the hell of the strong room and filing. It was Hale who opened the building in the morning and locked up last thing at night when everyone had gone. Not many people including the ever-knowledgeable Mrs Dailey knew whether he had any semblance of a normal life outside the office. In fact he was such a lifeless character that speculation was rarely rife. You hardly saw him, but you knew he was there. What was more, he was Mather's right-hand man.

The only real contact Peter had with him was when he received his monthly client and office account. Printed on green and white striped computer paper this would detail the debits or credits for each client account. Each fee earner within the firm received one. Since he had two or three hundred active files during any one month his was always a long document. He dreaded receiving his. He was no accountant and his invariably showed debits in some of his client accounts. This was the most heinous crime as far as the Law Society was concerned. He had been forced to go a refresher course that related the new stricter rules and regulations. Technically if you were one pound overdrawn on a client account you could be struck off. Even now he could see the book before him.

The guide to the Professional Conduct of Solicitors had haunted him for weeks after the course. Hale would ring any debits in red pen and scribble beside it what Peter had to do to correct it. Most of the time they were simply secretarial errors in filling out the necessary bank reconciliations. Sometimes they were more serious and every solicitor in the building could tell of a nightmare situation that brought the others out in a cold sweat. Peter often had visions of the Solicitors Complaints Bureau pouncing on his office at a moment's notice, confiscating all his files and suspending him. It annoyed him that like doctors and teachers his job was now hindered by endless number crunching and form filling which had little or nothing to do with the law and everything to do with mindless bureaucracy.

The other partners and assistants would arrive between 8.30 and 9.00 when the official working day began. It had always irked Peter that they were the only office in the city that opened up at 9.00. Almost all their rivals opened at 9.30. Mather had insisted on this time for years, stating that it gave them a competitive edge. It did not go unnoticed that Mather did not lead by example.

Peter was at his desk by 8.00 having dosed up on

caffeine and nicotine. By the time the office began to hum with activity he had finished a memo that Mather had demanded on the R.V Roland case. His work backlog was also looking much improved. He was pleased with himself. He had worked solidly for an hour. He had completely forgotten about the previous night and had instead submerged himself in a variety of legal problems.

For once he had used the computer to type up the memo to Mather. Paula, his secretary, did not arrive until 9.00. He did not quite understand the mechanics of how the thing printed. All he knew was that if he clicked the mouse on print twice, somewhere in the bowels of the building two copies would eventually be printed off. These would then make their way to the his tray in the post room where they would eventually be collected by Paula and returned to him with any other post for signing.

Once Paula had recuperated from her initial shock at seeing him in the office he dispatched her with alacrity to collect his masterpiece. Well, it was not a masterpiece as such but was sufficient to keep Mather quiet for a few days at least. He had decided to save the file under the original name of Roland on his terminal's hard drive. He still did not trust computers and if anything went wrong he would have a copy as evidence.

Paula returned a few minutes later with the memo. Checking it he signed his name to it. Handing her the audio tape and the files for the rest of the work that he had done he told her to put the memo into Mather's pigeon hole and tell him when he arrived. He told her not to place it on the top of the pile but to bury it under any other post. By the time Mrs Daley took it to him and he worked his way through everything else it might be mid-morning. He did not want to be pestered too early in the day.

At 9.30 Paula returned with his daily post and set about matching each letter with its corresponding file. It was at this point that he was reminded of Bobby Black, his very ex-client.

"Paula?" he asked. "Do you happen to remember any cases in which we acted for a Bobby Black?" She had an almost encyclopaedic knowledge of all the clients he had acted for. If anyone recalled anything in particular it would be her and she took her responsibility very seriously. She turned away from the filing cabinet she was rooting through. She furrowed her brow with deep concentration.

"The name rings a bell Peter, but I can't think of any specific matters we dealt with," she replied after a few minutes.

If she did not remember then he had little chance himself.

"Could you do me an enormous favour? I want you to pull all the old files on Bobby Black. I remember acting for him the first time. I was acting as duty solicitor. It must have been three years ago."

The job of filing dead files had been woefully neglected over the years, making it difficult to find anything, let alone a specific file. Finding a file therefore involved rooting around in hundreds of miscellaneous half-rotten piles of paper. Mather had called upon Hale to reorganise the whole system but still the stigma of such a task vexed the secretarial staff. Peter knew that it was a necessary task because under the Law Society rules, all law firms were obliged to keep all terminated case files for at least eight years.

"Isn't that Hale's department, why don't you request them from him?" she replied testily. Peter knew that all the secretaries were reluctant to do jobs that they believed fell into someone else's territory. It seemed that their job description involved them doing less and less as the years went by.

"Paula. You know how it is with him. He runs the basement like his own personal kingdom. By the time I've put in a memo requesting them and he's got round to pulling them, at least two weeks will have been wasted."

"How far back do you want me to go?" she asked reluctantly.

"Bring me everything." He paused. "And thank you very much Paula, I really do appreciate it. When I'm a little less busy I'll treat you to lunch at the Italian round the corner."

In spite of herself Paula smiled. He knew he was flirting with her slightly. The days of subservient staff had long gone and he believed you had to use every advantage God gave you. He knew his particular blessing was being able to flirt. Of course they both knew that he had no intention of honouring his lunch commitment.

"Okay," she said. "What about the computer records?" she continued.

He had forgotten that they had begun to store things on discs instead of taking up valuable space on the hard drive but he did not realise that they were kept. He could not think what relevant information would be on the discs so he asked her.

"Nothing much really. Any correspondence, that sort of thing. Since you don't use the computer much it would only be the work I have drafted. Just get me everything that you can. If they've kept the discs get me those as well."

"When do you want them? Am I right in thinking it's urgent?" she asked.

"This morning if possible." He knew he was really pushing his luck, but they had a good relationship and he knew that he could count on her in a crisis.

"I'll do my best," she said as she placed the post and files in front of him. "But don't be quick giving these back or I may turn nasty."

She laughed. He found himself laughing with her. "I don't want to be disturbed by anyone today Paula. okay?"

He needed time to think.

As she closed the door she said: "Oh, Mr Mather's in the building, been here since 9.30." Christ, Peter thought, he's early for the first time in years, he must be up to something. "He's probably looking forward to tearing me apart over the Roland case."

SIX

Martin Mather was master of all that he surveyed. At the age of fifty he was the senior partner of his own law firm with fourteen partners, twelve assistant solicitors, four trainee solicitors and eleven secretaries. Not one of the big solicitors' firms in the city, but one that had made a reputation for itself and more importantly which had survived the ravages of the recession virtually unscathed. He had taken over the four-partner firm twenty years ago.

He did not do, but delegated. He knew virtually nothing about the law and never had. He demanded success, basked in the reflected glory of any accomplishment and dished out punishment and blame for any failure. It was the failure of Peter Ritchie in the case of R.V. Roland that preoccupied him this morning. Mather could not begin to understand the complexities of the criminal law involved in the case, nor did he wish to. He did, however, understand the embarrassment and anger that he felt over the complaint that had been made by Mr Roland's brother on the telephone on Friday afternoon.

He had taken the call at four-fifteen, not realising who the caller was, and had mistaken the name given by his secretary as being Mr Bowler, a golfing partner of his. He had been out at a lunch meeting since twelve o' clock and had drunk the best part of a bottle of gin. The son of a poor Irish immigrant, hard drinking had always been a way of life for him.
"Good afternoon, George, how can I help you?" Mather had begun the conversation innocently.

"Is that Mr Mather, the senior partner? I'm Mr Roland," a confused Mr Roland had replied in a Hackney accent.

Mather, unaware that he had a client called Roland, replied. "Mr Roland who?"

"Mr Alistair Roland."

"And you are…?" Mather intoned sarcastically. He did not like to be disturbed.

"Alistair Roland, brother of your client Robert Roland in the case of R.V. Roland, the case your idiots lost leaving my brother to rot in prison." shouted Mr Roland angrily.

Mr Roland had then gone to complain about the service of Martin Mather and Co in their handling of the case, saying that Peter Ritchie had been incompetent from the beginning. Mather had eventually, after half an hour, managed to placate Mr Roland, giving his standard reply that he would investigate the matter himself and that if he cared to put the complaint in writing he would reply to him personally.

Mather could not understand why Peter Ritchie did not keep his head down like the other solicitors in the building. Ritchie was not a team player and he had no need for a rogue solicitor attracting the firm attention.

The problem was that Ritchie was a brilliant solicitor when he was firing on all cylinders and had the uncanny knack of bringing in lucrative clients for the firm. Ritchie had been threatened with the sack more times than Mather cared to remember over the last six years. He had reprimanded him and demanded that Ritchie deliver him a memo detailing the situation in the

R.V Roland case and the reasons they had lost the case, to him by 9.30am Monday morning. Unfortunately, it would take something more substantial to remove the thorn from his side.

Mather was distracted at this point by the appearance of his secretary, a short, fat, lazy woman. He had nothing against women but believed that they should concentrate on raising children and leave the work to the men. He had, due to more enlightened times, been forced to employ four female solicitors, of which two were partners in the firm, but always strongly resisted the employment of female trainee solicitors. He believed they would get married or pregnant and leave him to bear the cost of their training.
"Good morning Mrs Dailey," Mather crooned to his secretary with a vulpine smile.
"Where the bloody hell is Ritchie, he should have been in my office by now."

A fearful Mrs Dailey, who was well aware of Mather's rages whimpered that she had called his secretary who assured her he was on his way. Mather's lips curled into a smile, he always looked forward to reprimanding Ritchie. Mather had deliberately arrived at the office early. He had wanted to put the wind up Ritchie over the Roland matter.

It was therefore something of a surprise to learn that Peter Ritchie had been in the building since at least 8.30am. After dispensing with his minimum post and distributing anything more complicated to other fee earners Mrs Dailey had discovered the memo on the Roland case buried at the bottom of the tray. On its journey from

Ritchie's office to his pigeon hole the yellow carbon paper on which it was typed had become creased and folded at the edges. Holding it up like a piece of vital criminal evidence by one corner she had ceremoniously passed it to him.

It was almost a page long. What he wanted was a clear and concise statement of fact, not a rambling diatribe full of conjecture and attachment of blame to anyone other than Ritchie himself. It really maddened him that solicitors were not taught how to be lawyers anymore. Instead they were taught how to be diplomats and politicians, forever dodging the issue and avoiding the direct answering of questions. It was little wonder that most Members of Parliament had been or still were solicitors or barristers. Reading the memo he had seen that his first impression had been right. It was a beautifully constructed piece of creative writing that did nothing to enlighten him about the Roland case. He could have written the same memo in two precise lines. The evidence against Roland was overwhelming and the judge had decided that he would do everything in his power to see that he was found guilty. Ritchie had formulated the best defence that he could in light of this evidence and had achieved the best result available to him. He knew that this was the case because he had talked to the judge personally when they had lunched together at the RAC in Pall Mall.

The other thing that was bothering him was the Bobby Black matter. He had seen the news last night detailing Bobby's death. It was not the fact that Bobby had died that bothered him, it was the fact that he had been a client of his firm. Coming from the old school he hated any whiff of a scandal. He had a blanket policy of refusing to act for potentially newsworthy clients. Like a giant corporate turtle they would pull their neck into the shell at the vaguest hint of trouble. He, unlike many people, believed that all publicity was bad publicity. It would turn the spotlight of attention on them and might scare away some of his bigger clients who felt comfortable with the low profile existence of the firm.

He had been hiding, as he always did from his domestic life, in the comfort of his study, enjoying a glass of gin and tonic. Waiting until everyone was in bed before he ventured out. He had no control over his personal life. He could exert none of the power that he wielded at work, leaving him feeling impotent, powerless, subject to the dominance of his overbearing wife who ruled the house with a rod of iron.

He had watched the news unfold with detachment, unaware that the few minutes of news accorded to one of his firm's clients was of any relevance at all. Enjoying the last few sips of his last large gin and tonic of the night before venturing upstairs.
Hale had phoned him moments after the news had ended. He had been quick to pick up the call, he did not want to wake his wife. She would make his life hell if a late-night call disturbed her beauty sleep. Their conversation had been short and to the point.

He was not surprised to hear from Hale. It was not a habit, but he had phoned on occasion when a crisis was emerging. Hale had not said much. It was enough that a known prostitute had been a client of theirs, a prostitute who had been murdered and was subject of media speculation. He had finished by saying that they would discuss it further in the morning. First thing in the morning.

It was no surprise that Ritchie was involved. Ritchie seemed to attract the wrong sort of people.

Once the post was finished and he had dismissed Mrs Dailey he settled down to enjoy the rest of his morning. He had just spread the Times out on the desk when his phone rang. It was Hale. The eyes, ears, nose, throat and rectum of the company. It was not the official agenda that he should assume this role. Mather had never commanded him to do so. None of the partners had. Put simply, Hale had a unique position with access to all fee earners accounts and past files, side by side with general timekeeping data. He did not have to act in an underhand manner to discover facts that the other partners were isolated from by the very nature of their power within the infrastructure. This information was at his fingertips at all times. At partners meetings he would be called upon to talk at length about how each fee earner was doing. He would identify weaknesses and update on what they all called 'Hot Files'.

He did not see this as spying or the Big Brother approach. Hale was merely fulfilling his personification of the perfect managing partner. The others were pleased to delegate this tedious and time-consuming role to someone else, someone who clearly enjoyed his chosen role, and he more than earned his inflated salary. Outside of the monthly partners meetings Mather rarely saw or spoke to Hale. He did not think much of him as a person. Then again he did not think much of any of his fellow partners. That was not important to Martin Mather.

"Good morning Martin," Hale opened the conversation. "I trust that you are well."
"What can I do for you?" Mather was not in the mood for polite chit chat.
"What are we going to do about the Black matter?" Hale asked.
"I remember nothing about him, this is your department. If he had been important I am sure I would have recalled something. No one can connect us with the case and if they do, what can we tell them?
"Well that's just it. I do not think we could either. But what about Ritchie? He may know something. Discretion can be counted on from the others but I cannot speak for him. As you yourself described him, he is something of a loose cannon."
"I will see him later and put him straight on a few things. What could he do anyway? I do not suppose he even knows about it yet," Mather countered.
"He's requested all the dead files and disc data," Hale responded.
This set off alarm bells within Mather's head. If he wanted the files and discs he must want them for a specific reason. Ritchie was a maverick but he was also a fine lawyer.
"Are you aware of anything in them? Were they hot?" Mather continued.
The partners had a system whereby Hale would code certain files as hot if they might prove potentially embarrassing to the firm or more to

the point the client. No one outside the partners knew about this system. There was no need for anyone else to know.

"To be honest I don't know. Looking at my screen I can see only four matters. An advice given at the police station, a Power of Attorney, instructions for a will and a further meeting that has been listed as a miscellaneous private client matter. Oh and we also have his original will in our strong room. None of them were hot and I cannot imagine that the discs hold anything more than a few copy documents and correspondence."

Mather smiled. Hale was, as usual, one step ahead. This was why they had appointed him managing agent. He made a mental note to recommend a suitable reward when the partners next met.

If the files were not hot then he could see no reason why Ritchie could not have them. What harm could it do? He would find nothing in them of any relevance, nothing that could possibly have any bearing on his murder. But first he had to be sure.

"It must just be idle curiosity then." Even as he said this Mather knew that few solicitors acted on idle curiosity, Ritchie even less so.

"What does worry me is the fact that Ritchie bypassed the usual request system. He asked his secretary to get them urgently. She is waiting for them now." Hale continued with more than an intimation of scepticism in his voice. Hale did not like anyone deviating from the accepted practice.

"I will speak to him myself on this one. Just to see

what he is up to." He planned to speak to him about Roland anyway.

Ritchie would be expecting him and he was not going to march into his office straight away. He was going to make him worry about it. And then he would summon him. He knew there was nothing to worry himself about. But years of practice had made him highly suspicious. He hoped that he would not live to regret his decision to allow Ritchie to see the files.

SEVEN

Categorically, Peter could state that, so far, the day had been an unmitigated disaster. Litigation, as every solicitor knew, was not an exact science. Things happened that no one could control, no matter how brilliant they were. Juggling the ever-ubiquitous needs of the client with the backlog of necessary and urgent, ominously piled up paperwork was never a smooth process. All litigators could point at a file that could be considered eminently urgent and imminently waiting!

Criminal Litigation was made yet more haphazard by the nature of the fact that any case generally involved the liberty of individuals. It involved a game of double jeopardy. One piece of mail could alter the status of a case and give it an edge that previously did not exist.

Peter thought that he was being punished in some perverse way for arriving at the office early. The half dozen letters Paula have given him earlier in the morning had nuclear consequences for all the clients involved. Not all of it was negative, some was positive, but it all had one thing in common they all required hours of attention that he did not have.

In the Palmer case his client was charged with Actual Bodily Harm and he had received the Crown Prosecution bundle of documents for the trial. A complicated case involving the assault of a former nightclub bouncer with a baseball bat, it consisted of twelve detailed witness statements, four arresting officer statements, a record of the tape-recorded interview and the police record of his previous convictions.

Reading these had proved time-consuming enough and it was almost midday before he finished identifying any opinion, hearsay and similar fact evidence that could be excluded from the bundle. Although the instructed barrister would, no doubt, want to argue with him over the exclusions, it nevertheless, remained his policy to attempt to exclude everything that he thought was suspect and hope that the prosecution would agree. If not they would have to reason it out in front of the judge. This would, naturally, lengthen the trial and upset the judge who would have to send the jury out. He also had to examine his client's statements to him to see how the two emerging stories tallied - they seldom did. Most of his criminal clients suffered from a form of amnesia when telling their side of the sorry tale and nine times out of ten they omitted material facts. Facts that spun at the epicentre of their case.

Another letter told him that a key witness in a theft trial had disappeared off the face of the earth. They had tried to trace him and had resorted to serving a witness summons on his last known address requiring him to attend court on the trial day. He had a statement from him. That was not the problem. Normally such evidence would be admissible under Section 23 of the Criminal Justice Act 1988 unless various criteria were fulfilled. He knew that these criteria were fulfilled and he could present the written statement to open court. The problem was that in his experience the jury rarely listened to anything read to them.

Taking a breather for another cigarette he had
time to reflect on the events of the previous night.
He instantly tensed up again when he thought of
Bobby's body lying on a cold sheet of metal in the
morgue. Then he remembered that the autopsy
was due to take place this morning. Naomi had,
as always, been the voice of reason. He had told
her everything in bed. She had said that he had
nothing to reproach himself for. He could not have
prevented the inevitable. He knew that she was
right but still he took no solace from her words.
She did nothing to dispel the disquiet that was
struggling to find substance within the convoluted
jumble of thoughts in his mind.

It was at this point that the phone on his desk
rang, breaking his thought pattern. He did not
know it then, but this was to be one of those
twists of fate that most people scoff at. Picking up
the phone he discovered it was Paula.

Paula was normally very adept at fiddling calls
and had invented a catalogue of excuses that
would shame the most ardent of liars.

"I thought you'd want to speak to him. He said it
was to do with the Black case. Since you asked for
all the old files I guessed you would be
interested," Paula explained.
He sat bolt upright in his chair.
He was interested. "Who is it?" He did not think it
could be Brown.
"He says his name is Bowers. It doesn't mean
anything to me."
He could not place the name for a moment and

then he remembered. The mortuary assistant. Peter had never expected him to actually call. "I want to speak to him. Before you put me through, where are those files I asked for?" Paula replied, "I've got them here. I'll bring them in after you have finished if you like." "Thanks Paula." He listened as Paula put Bowers through. On the cue of the connecting click he spoke. After years of practice he managed to remove all traces of anticipation from his voice.

"Good afternoon Mr Bowers." "Hello Mr Ritchie". Bowers was speaking very quietly as if he did not want to be overheard. Peter thought he could hear hospital noises in the background. "I'll get straight to the point. I haven't got much time and what I'm doing could ruin my medical career, not to mention my life. I don't want you to think that this is something I do all the time. This is strictly a one-off. If this blows up in your face I don't want this getting back to me. Do I make myself clear?" Bowers continued.

"Perfectly." He wanted to keep it simple so that Bowers could speak uninterrupted. "I saw the news reports of his death last night. I knew that the autopsy would be important but..." Peter noted that his voice was rising with arousal. Each word seemed to be charged with an electric thrill.

"The autopsy followed standard procedure. Didn't expect them to find anything. None of us did. The police had said that they were not looking for anyone else. It was when the pathologist was examining the neck that things changed."

"What do you mean?" Peter could not resist asking the question.

"Normally with autoerotic strangulation the marks on the neck caused by the pressure of the cord would have subsided slightly by the following day."

"Why?" Peter asked.

"The whole point of autoerotic strangulation is that at the point of orgasm the cord tightens around the throat, cutting off the oxygen supply, therefore restricting the flow of blood to the brain. Thus heightening the sense of orgasm. In cases like this, where the loosening of the cord relies on someone else releasing the pressure, that moment comes too late. The airway has been restricted to such a degree that effectively they are slowly asphyxiated."

Peter felt very uncomfortable at this thought and wondered what kind of sick pervert would indulge such a pastime.

"So?" It had all been a horrible accident, the sad outcome of a sex game gone wrong.

"Effectively there is little significant damage to the bones, muscle or tissue of the neck region. What we found was not consistent with the known facts. On examining the neck region we discovered some haemorrhaging to the strap muscles, the thyroid was partially fractured and there were some small fractures to the superior horns of the thyroid cartilage."

Peter did not understand what the technical jargon indicated.

"Explain this to me in slow, plain English. I'm not a doctor."

Bowers continued "there is no indication that Black was not a willing participant in the act itself. No physical signs of a struggle. Fact is, he probably allowed this to be done to him, maybe he even enjoyed it. It appears however that whoever was with him decided to take it a stage further. Instead of loosening the ligature when it became evident that Black was passing out, he tightened it. Tightened it so much that it strangled him. Anyone normal would have realised that they were strangling him. This person, whoever he was, just carried on applying more and more pressure. Black more than likely did not know what was happening and even if he did, in his weakened state he couldn't have done anything about it."

Peter was still uneasy about whether Bobby would have participated in such an act.
"Could he have been drugged? Strangled with the ligature and then set up to look like this?"
"That's a possibility, we're still waiting for the toxicology report. But I think it's unlikely, especially given Black's chosen profession," Bowers replied.

"Personally, I would have thought that would make it more likely. There are some sick people out there." Peter paused to assimilate all the information he had received.
"What you are saying is that he was murdered. If I understand you correctly?"

"Yea." They were both silent for few minutes and the word murdered seemed to hang in the air between them.
"Listen Ritchie I'd better go. I've been on the phone long enough."

"Thanks for calling me Mr Bowers. Will you let me know the results of the toxicology report?"

"Yea." Now Bowers had confessed all, he seemed to have little else to say.

"Tell me. Why did you call me?" Peter knew that Bowers must have some sort of motive. It clearly wasn't money or he would have gone straight to the press. What else could it be?

"Because you said he was your friend."

Before he could say any more Bowers put the phone down.

EIGHT

Once dressed in his finest Saville Row suit, Charles Church shoes, guards' tie and brilliant white shirt, Justin Gordon Hodge headed down to breakfast.

As he entered the dining room he realised another reason why he could consider himself in a foul temper. Sitting at one end of the dining table was his wife Lady Lavinia Hodge. It had been her fault that he had to travel to the marital home. He had been summoned the night before. This was something she had not done on more than half a dozen occasions during the last fifteen years of their thirty-year marriage. Looking at the woman before him now he felt a momentary sadness for his wife. Things could have been so different when they first met. They had both been so full of hope. At sixty she was still beautiful, elegant and refined. But that did not change the fact that things had gone too far. They were beyond redemption. An icy wedge, that could not be thawed, had been driven between them for years.

He marched to the sideboard to help himself to breakfast.
"Good morning Lavinia. I trust that you slept well."
She looked up at him from her end of the table with nothing but naked hatred in her opaque eyes. "To what do I owe this honour Justin. It is rare to see you at my table on a Monday morning, or any other morning for that matter."

To an untrained ear she would sound normal. Anyone else would hear only the hatred. He heard something else, something she hid well.

The judge helped himself to some toast and coffee from the sideboard prepared and laid out by the housekeeper, and returned to sit at the opposite end of the table. A large table, Regency, if he remembered correctly, with twelve matching Regency chairs arranged with two ornate carvers at either end and six chairs either side. It was a magnificent room with high Georgian ceilings and ornate cornices. Two vast chandeliers dripping in crystals hung from gold chains hung ceremoniously above the middle of the table. When he was at the Grange, both he and Lavinia chose to sit in the carvers. It seemed to signify the distance that separated them now and prevented him being within easy firing range. As the years had worn on so to had her desire to throw heavy objects in his direction.

From some distance he scrutinised his wife, she looked far younger than her true age despite the forces that had raged within her body unchecked for years. He noticed that as usual she was not having any solids for breakfast, instead favouring a liquid diet. An antique claret jug sporting her family crest was within reach. Filled with fresh martinis.

His wife had become increasingly tiresome to him in the last few years. At first she had accepted the arrangement and fulfilled herself with odd job men, handymen and gardeners, her charity work and the Women's Institute. He had always kept an eye on the man of the moment, dispensing with any opportunists, scandalmongers or favoured toy boys with a suitably large cheque from Lavinia's bank account. He did not want his wife to either leave him or cause any damage to his career. Other than that he did not care how she filled her spare time.

The last serious Romeo had proved to be a thorn in his side. George Brabon the chauffeur had professed undying love to Lavinia, they had planned to run off together. The judge had dealt with the situation in his usual way. He had offered the man £100,000 in an unmarked Swiss bank account. George had prevaricated for a few weeks and then accepted the sum. Love is blind, the judge thought wryly. George had left that day never to return. He never explained why he left Lavinia nor left any clues as to his whereabouts.

The judge of course knew where he was. Knew exactly what had happened to him. He had arranged it all. He felt a slight pang of guilt. How could he have known what would happen? That had been ten years ago. Lavinia had not taken a lover since.

After George's disappearance she had begun to seek solace in uppers and downers, sleeping pills and finally alcohol. He did not care what she did with her time as long as she kept out of his way and he was happy to pay. She never appeared to be any the worse for wear for her chosen excesses and if anything a marked improvement had taken place recently.
"I do not suppose for one minute that you recall last night?" They had to talk loudly due to the length of the table. Lavinia downed another martini in one gulp. Averting her eyes, as if she could not bear to look at him.
"What are you bloody talking about?"

"Language, Lavinia. I am talking about the phone call you made to me last night at about 11.00pm, stating that you were going to kill yourself. Any vague recollection yet?"

She retorted that he was mad, she had no idea to what he was referring to.

"This has got to stop, Lavinia. It is a very important year for me. If things go according to plan I shall be elevated to the law lords. Any whiff of a scandal will destroy my chances. I do not want to cover old ground this morning. I have tried to make you see. If you keep torturing yourself you will make yourself ill."

"What do you care, Justin? Tell me that. What do you care? What could I possibly do that would harm your precious career?"

Commit suicide, he thought. This was the only threat she held over him now. He regretted this almost as soon as he thought it. He would not have her death on his conscience as well. If she did kill herself he wanted to stave off the inevitable at least until after his appointment to the House of Lords, when he could at least carry out a programme of damage limitation and play the grieving widower. If it happened before his chances of appointment were slim.

He was also concerned that in her drunken state she might reveal a little too much about their arrangement and, more to the point, the few scant but potentially explosive things that she knew about his exile in Belgravia. She had always suspected the worst anyway, but in true British stiff upper lip fashion had ignored it. They had never spoken about it. She had never even tried, but she knew. The irony of the Roland case was not lost on him. It was, however, overpowered by his all-consuming arrogance and conviction that he still had the right to sit in moral judgement over lesser mortals who did not have the powerful friends and protection that he enjoyed.

"Lavinia. I am telling you for the last time that this attention seeking will not work. I have instructed Mrs Walker not to allow you near the phone and if it carries on, the martini rations you so enjoy will be cut again."

If she was determined to behave like a child then he had no choice but to treat her like one. It had been a gamble but it had worked. Saying nothing, she defiantly poured herself a large martini from the jug and downed it in one swift movement. Realising that his position was hopeless, the judge leaned across the table and, picking up the handbell, gave it one firm ring. Mrs Walker opened the door of the dining room a few moments later.

A statuesque figure, he could not help feel that she would be as at home as a warden in a women's prison as she was in the Grange. She had been sacked in dubious circumstances from an institution. Something about an incident involving one of the female prisoners. He did not want to know the details. Desperation breeds loyalty of all varieties and there was no question of where her loyalties lay. She told him everything he needed to know. Lavinia treated her contemptuously, suspicious of her true purpose for being in the house. But she had no choice but to keep her on. Because she also fulfilled another design. That of dishing out the pills and martini to which she had become inextricably connected. Drugs which only he could supply through a friendly doctor in Harley Street, who handed out prescriptions like confetti and, more importantly, asked no questions.

Mrs Walker, will you take Lady Hodge upstairs for her morning nap? Make sure you cut back on her pills as she is more unreasonable than usual today."
"Very good sir."

The judge got up from his table and headed out of the room as Mrs Walker began to manoeuvre his wife into a standing position. Unable to watch the pitiful sight of his wife being manhandled the judge started to make his exit.
"Bastard."
Unseen by him, a crystal glass flew through the air and shattered against the top of the door, showering the judge in shards of glass. He did not even look round. He was used to such displays of affection from his wife and merely brushed the glass fragments from his hair and clothing as he left.
In the car, driving to London he thought about his wife, Lavinia. It had been different when they had first met. It had been 1955 and he had reached a stumbling block in his career.

He had attended Eton College on a scholarship, his poor family could not afford the fees and his father had been dead for years by then. He had proved himself to be a brilliant and able student. At eighteen he had gained a place at Cambridge University studying law, finishing his three years with a first class degree and the top marks in his year. The Second World War had begun in 1939, one year into his studies. He had considered this a minor irritant to his inevitably brilliant career and, joining the air force, he had served with distinction until the end of hostilities. He had nothing against heroism. It was simply that if he was killed it would deprive the world of one of the greatest legal minds of the twentieth century. His contribution was too important to ignore.

After the interlude of the war years he had then gone to Bar school, where he again attained top honours, joining the chambers of Alan Campbell QC for his two years pupillage and for the following years until his ascendancy into the ranks of the judiciary. At thirty he was appointed Queens Counsel after submitting his name to the Lord Chancellor for consideration and upon approval being appointed by the Queen. He then proceeded to dominate all the landmark criminal defence cases for the next fifteen years. It was at this point that he realised that his career had stagnated. If he was to get a judicial position he had to marry and the ideal opportunity appeared before him in the form of Lavinia.

He had been at yet another boring cocktail party at a colleague's house in Belgravia one evening after work. She looked awkward in the cocktail dress that clung to her a la mode frame. Her auburn hair was a messy parody of the latest fashion and her face was handsome rather than beautiful. Her eyes though, were the most comely green, sparkling with wit and intelligence. She somehow appeared worldly beyond her twenty years.

She, like him, was shy and largely withdrawn from other people. Apparently, he learned later, she had been watching him all night from the other side of the room and was fascinated by his moody good looks. He of course had not noticed her at all, though he pretended that he had when she asked. He did not spend his time looking for women and she had mistaken his indifference for a man who was used to the attention of women. She reminded him of his mother as he had imagined her to be when she had been young. By the end of the party they had swapped telephone numbers and promised to get in touch.

In the following few months he saw her almost every day and to her it must have seemed like a courtship. To him it was nothing more than a business partnership. Within two months of meeting her he had proposed to Lavinia. He made it perfectly clear that theirs was to be nothing more than an arrangement. She, it seemed, had never truly understood the nature of their marriage.

He was marrying her for her money and position in order to smooth his career path. She was marrying him because no one else would. They had never slept together, he had seen to it. Soon after they married he had purchased 'the Grange' and the mews house with her money and had issued strict instruction that he was to live in Belgravia alone and that on no account was she ever to visit him. The Grange was for her to live in, and he would only visit when necessary for social functions or if she invited him. He also made it clear that she was a free agent. She had no fear of recriminations from him for any indiscretions that she might embark upon. This, as he was to discover, was not strictly true.

He returned his thoughts to the Roland case. Things had gone better than expected and he had completed his summing-up in a record forty minutes, which for a six-day trial was pretty spectacular. He had given the jury all the necessary warnings and guidance on the law and had then summed-up the evidence of both the prosecution and defence in turn. The jury could not have been left in any question as to the correct verdict.

The jury had returned in thirty minutes, a sure sign that they had found the defendant guilty. He had been elated and thanked the jury for acting so expeditiously in a grave and complicated case, especially as they had done so before lunch. He had revelled in the laughter that had reverberated around the court. There were no other cases listed for the day, leaving him free to enjoy a lengthy lunch at his club, the Royal Automobile Club in Pall Mall.

His thoughts drifted back to his wife. It frustrated him that he could not control her completely. His visit to her house had unnerved him. Up until then she had appeared to have called a truce in the never-ending battle that their marriage had become. The truce had begun subtly, though it was so subtle that he only realised that it had happened with hindsight. Her behaviour at breakfast had signalled an end to that uneasy peace.

He wondered if she had embarked on yet another

reckless affair. He had come to recognise the signs over the years and there was no denying that she was still an attractive woman. He knew all the signs. He determined to find out who it was. He would find out. But this time he would not make the same mistake. He was no doubt attracted to her wealth. Wealth that had always been, would continue to be, a magnet to prospectors.

Suddenly he was jolted from his reverie by the phone ringing on his desk. He took a deep breath and walked to the desk, picking up the phone. "Yes, what is it?" he barked down the phone. It was his clerk. "Sorry to disturb you, Your Honour. There is a man on the phone. A reporter from the Daily Mail. I tried to tell him that you were not available, but he was most insistent that you would want to hear what he said. I said that you were out to lunch but he knew that you had not left yet".

Sighing with annoyance, he sat back down heavily in his chair.
"You really must try to be more convincing. Oh, very well, I will take the call".
The judge was a very high-profile figure and was often pestered by the press for quotes on controversial cases. He pretended to be annoyed but was, in fact, deeply flattered. Although he did not understand why the case of R.V. Roland would be of any particular interest to members of the press. This was after all only a very trivial case. His next case however was a murder trial. Perhaps they wanted his comments on that. He could of course make no comment, but he did not see any harm in talking to him.

"Good morning, Your Honour". The caller's voice was heavily disguised, sexless, mechanical, computer generated.

He was unnerved.

The voice explained he was a friend, he'd been watching the R.V Roland case from the gallery. The voice explained

"I'm not a reporter, Your Honour."

The judge was angry "I am going to put the phone down now and then inform security".

Security was normally very tight around the building. He would have them trace the call. The judge moved to put the receiver down when he heard the mystery caller say something. Not sure that he heard him properly he froze as he felt the colour drain from his face. He suddenly felt ill. "What did you say?" he asked weakly.

The mystery voice paused for thought before continuing "How is your wife coping at 'the Grange' Your Honour, does she know what you get up to in your mews house?"

The judge gripped the edge of the table as he began to feel faint and the room began to spin before his eyes. This was something he had feared would happen for many years. He had to find out what the voice at the end of the phone knew.

He retorted with as much bravado as he could muster "I do not believe for a minute that you know anything." The mechanical voice chuckled ominously down the phone.

"Please, Your Honour, give me some credit. I was watching your house last Wednesday at about twelve pm. I've got some very interesting photographs. Quite exciting if you like that sort of thing. Personally I find it disgusting and feel that it is my moral duty to expose, do forgive the pun, Your Honour, the peccadilloes of people in the public eye."

Within seconds it came to him. Fear swept through him and he had to fight an urge to pass out at his desk. Placing the receiver on the desk, bending down to the waste-paper basket to the right of the desk, he was suddenly and silently sick. The world went blank. For a few moments he could not remember anything.

Sitting bolt upright in his chair, he fumbled in his trouser pocket for the crisp linen handkerchief that he knew was there. Unfolding it, he carefully dabbed the corners of his mouth to remove the dribbles of warm sick he felt running down his chin. He knew exactly what he had been doing on Wednesday night. It had never happened there before. He had always been so careful. A moment of madness.
Composing himself, he picked up the receiver, listening for the voice.
"I'm sorry if you feel ill Your Honour, but I had to prove that I knew things. That you would take me seriously. You see I'm not your ordinary blackmailer."

How did he know he had been sick, the judge thought. Can he see me? The judge whipped his head around the room to see if this was the case, but there was no possibility of him seeing into his chambers. He must have heard me being sick he decided.
"How much do you want?"
The mechanical voice laughed again. "It's not

money that I'm after, Your Honour."
"Then what?" the judge pleaded.
"When the time is right I'll tell you. In the meantime, Your Honour, it has been a pleasure talking to you. I'll be watching you. Adios, amigo." The phone went dead.

The judge sat back in his chair. He did not feel well at all, he could feel beads of sweat breaking out on his forehead, sheathing his body beneath his clothes. He had been exposed at last. How did all this begin? He could remember it as if it was yesterday. It had begun when he was at Eton in 1933. Sixty-two years ago. If only he had never gone there, maybe, maybe it would have changed things. Altered the course of history.

His father had been dead for three years when he had won a church scholarship. He had not wanted to leave his mother. She was his world. His brothers and sisters, who were much older than him, had long since left home. He despised them because they had left him alone with their father. They were all dead now, he had not mourned them, to him they were nothing.

"A young man rises or falls on the strength of his education Justin. You must go." And so at the tender age of thirteen, haunted by the unresolved memories of his father, he had been dispatched to Eton. A difficult child, his only friend had been his mother, and out of stubborn objection he had refused to enjoy it. Vowing to keep himself to himself he made few companions or friends. He had quickly become the butt of his fellow pupils' jokes and pranks. They had teased him about his poor background.

He remembered Humphrey. The prefect to whom he had been assigned as study fag within the first few days. His tasks were simple and endless. He was at the beck and call of Humphrey both day and night. Cleaning his study, making him tea, washing his rugby kit, waking him in the mornings, buying things from the tuck shop. He remembered endless and brutal beatings for minor misdemeanours and the simple sadistic pleasure that this would instil in Humphrey. In the recess of his mind he knew something else about Humphrey but it had been so many years ago, could that really have any bearing on his life now? But that was when it had all started and now here he was, with his past finally catching up with him.

NINE

At three o' clock Peter received an internal call requesting his presence in the colonel's office, immediately. The colonel was Mather's nickname. He ruled with a rod of iron and behaved as if he had been in the army, when in fact he had done his few years of national service along with all his other contemporaries before opting for the equally vicious world of law.

Having been in the office since the crack of dawn, Peter had thought that he had escaped unscathed from the Randal debacle. He headed for the top floor. Mrs Dailey showed him into the conference room next to Mather's office.

He was happy to wait in the conference room. It was a room that he rarely saw, reserved for impressing clients and for the mysterious gathering of the partners once a week. It was a magnificent room, decorated in antique splendour, portraying silently and elegantly the firm's history and significance. It would reassure the most sceptical of potential clients of the firm's ability. The conference room was dominated by a huge Victorian dining table, the mahogany buffed over the years to a glass-like shine.

Around the table sat ten matching chairs and, at either end, two ornate carver chairs. Peter could imagine the partners huddled around the table conspiratorially, with the colonel and Hale sitting, bloated with self-importance, in the two carvers. The only way he would ever make it to the lofty heights of partnership was if they were both killed concurrently in some hideous accident. He had his supporters amongst the partners, but he also had his detractors, most critically in the person of the senior partner, who would rather see hell freeze over than allow him a place at his table.

Peter decided to sit in the colonel's chair while he waited. While he waited, it occurred to him that, throughout his life, he had been summoned to meetings like this. He could not help but clash with whoever was in authority. His parents must have wondered whether they had brought the wrong child home from hospital. As soon as he could walk Peter had begun to rebel against his parents' quiet middle-class ways.

It became such a problem that they were forced to move him from preparatory school to preparatory school throughout Surrey in the vain hope that he would settle somewhere. Each expulsion brought further embarrassment for his parents, but no reprisals, and years later Peter would conclude that this was ultimately what he was after. It was not that they did not love him, they did. They were strangled by their conservative middle-class values. They both struggled to show any emotion.

They provided a stable home for their only son and gave him everything that was within their means. Charles his father had been the manager of the Surbiton branch of the National Westminster Bank until his early retirement at fifty-nine in 1994. Even this had annoyed Peter. His father had not so much retired as been retired when the bank in its wisdom and rationalisation of the nineties decided that managers were no longer necessary. Charles had accepted this without the faintest hint of bitterness.

What they failed to see was that he had never
been a rebel, he had simply stood up for the
underdog. At all his schools he had become the
spokesman for his classmates, he had stood up
for their rights.

While he was scrutinising the chandelier Mather
quietly appeared at the door. He did not realise he
was there until it was too late.
"Good afternoon Ritchie."

Not the most auspicious of starts Peter thought as
he almost jumped out of Mather's chair.
"If I could have my chair. I think we shall talk in
here. It's less formal than my office, don't you
think?" Mather continued.
This automatically worried Peter. For one thing
the conference room was not less formal than his
office. Secondly Peter knew that only the most
serious matters were dealt with here. Getting up
quietly and confidently, hiding his nerves, Peter
moved around one place to his left.

Mather's piercing grey eyes seemed to bore into
the back of Peter's head. He was still smiling.
"I'll get straight to the point Peter." He had never
called him by his first name. "What exactly do you
see as your future at Mather & Co?"

Peter was further thrown off his guard. He had
not expected this to be the topic of conversation
and he feared the worst. A pep talk leading to an
unfortunate and regrettable dismissal.

"Well sir, like anyone, one day I would like to be a
partner. In fact sir if I may speak bluntly?" He did

not wait for Mather's reply but kept talking. "I feel that I have already served my apprenticeship and am more than able and qualified to assume such a role. I have always consistently billed more than my contemporaries and in the last few years I have increased it."

"No one can argue with the figures Peter and in that respect we have always acknowledged your achievements. To be a partner is more than billable hours, you have to be part of a team Peter. You have to be a team player and that is where you have failed yourself. You are a loose cannon aboard a tight ship. Again and again you insist on acting in a kamikaze and cavalier manner with no regard for the well-being of the firm."

Peter interrupted him. "Should we, should I, abandon all my principles just so that I can be part of a team?"
"Peter come now who are we to talk of principles? I am simply telling you how it is. Maybe you are playing for the wrong team." He paused and looked Peter in the eye
"In short if you refuse to toe the line maybe it would be mutually beneficial to all parties if you were to look for employment elsewhere."

He knew damn well that with the recession still biting firmly into the legal world he would struggle to find another job. Peter knew that he would have to agree with Mather even if it galled him to do so. They both knew he had no choice.
"I don't think we need discuss the Roland case any further. That is simply the most recent of your failures. I'm still not happy with the way you

handled it but, given the facts and the client himself, I don't think we will take it any further. You will hand the case over to Jenkins who will deal with it from now on. What I am clear on is the fact that Ms Brahman must no longer act for this firm in any of your cases, do I make myself clear?"

Jenkins was a young whiz kid who had joined the firm three years ago and was now Peter's immediate superior. Jenkins was the favourite amongst the partners for early elevation to the top floor, something which vexed Peter.

"Sir I do not think we need to be that hasty. Miss Brahman is one of the more able and competent barristers in her chambers. It would in my opinion be very unfortunate if we had to dispense with her services entirely."

Mather responded without hesitation "That may be the case but I'm not asking you to consider this as an option. I'm telling you the way it will be. As far as I see it she was ill-prepared and advised the client badly. I appreciate that you have developed a working relationship but we cannot carry incompetence. After all, our first duty is to the client, not the instructed barrister."

Peter knew instantly what Mather's game was. He was deftly shifting the blame. If any faults were to be found in their provision of legal services they would be firmly laid at Naomi's feet. He probably did not believe this any more than Peter but he was protecting the firm's name from any potential fallout.

"Sir. Even if there was a potential problem with this case, which I don't think there is, Naomi, I mean Miss Brahman pitched the best defence available in the circumstances. In most cases we brief her on, we ultimately answer to the higher authority of the Legal Aid Board," Peter countered.

This was not strictly true but he was counting on Mather's general ignorance of legal aid procedure to win the argument. "What exactly do you mean?" Mather had taken the bait. "Well sir, without lecturing to you at length on legal aid procedure with which I am sure you are more than accustomed, most of my cases are legally aided. You know as well as I do that ultimately the board will not remove an instructed barrister from the legal aid certificate without good reason. If she were to convince them that she should not be discharged they would not do so. Especially as most of the cases are at an advanced stage. The client himself can rarely sack his solicitors without their authority, which due to prohibitive costs they are extremely unlikely to grant."

He paused, if he could not persuade him on procedural grounds he certainly could ascertain the financial pressure. Mather was silent so he continued "besides they would not extend legal aid to include the necessary preparatory work a new barrister would have to carry out. Either the clients would have to fund this themselves, which most of them cannot, or we would find those costs our responsibility," he concluded.

He wanted the financial burden that this would place on the firm's resources to sink in. He knew that no partner, let alone the senior partner, would ever spend money unnecessarily. The unwritten rule in all solicitors firms was that you did nothing unless someone was paying for your time. Even the most morally adjusted solicitor refused to act unless either the client or the legal aid fund agreed to cover their costs. If a client was serious he would hand over at least one thousand pounds in advance. If he could not pay, the solicitor would apply for legal aid. If he did not receive aid the case would advance no further, no matter how cast iron it was. To do anything else would cut into the profit margins for each and every one of the partners and ultimately the world of justice had to rely on profit margins in order to survive. There were no Robin Hood's in the legal world.

Mather sat quietly as he thought this through. "Very well. She can continue on those cases she is already instructed on, except the Roland case which still goes to Jenkins. And you are not to instruct her on any new matters, is that clear?" Mather said grudgingly.

Peter sensed the feeling of a minor victory rise in him. He would tackle the matter of further instructions at a later date. "Thank you sir." Peter tried not to sound triumphant. "Moving on Peter. I noticed that one of your clients, Bobby Black, was found dead last night. If there is any flak connected to this I do not want you to have anything to do with it. You know the policy of the firm. We do not get involved in controversial or sensational cases. Our clients rely on us for discretion and tact, any publicity would be bad for the firm." He spoke reasonably but firmly.

Peter was shocked by the sudden change of subject. The colonel was not always unaware of the world around him. Peter suspected that Hale must have jolted his memory by telling him that the files had been requested. Peter was not sure how to deal with the subject. Rejecting lying, he decided to tell him the truth. However, he was not about to recount the phone call from Bowers. He would not lie, but he would only say what had to be said.

Starting at the beginning he told him about his visit to the morgue to identify the body. Mather sat motionless, unmoved throughout. Peter remained prosaic as he spoke. As if the whole thing was totally tedious to him. "I have ordered the files from Hale because, put simply, my curiosity was pricked and I thought there might be some work in it for me or at least the probate department," Peter finished.

Mather responded "I happen to know that you personally drafted a will for him some years ago. I do not know what it contained. But even if we have been appointed as executors I do not want you getting involved. Hand it over to the Wills and Probate department."

Peter knew that the colonel could not possibly know anything about the case unless Hale had told him. He had forgotten about the will himself, although he now remembered that he had drafted it on Bobby's insistence. Hopefully the files would be back on his desk when he got back and he could investigate the matter further.

He told Mather "I do not honestly know what files we have. I have not seen them yet. However if you tell me that's what we did then you must be right.

Could I ask you sir where you got this information?" he knew where the information had come from, he simply wanted to put him on the spot.

Peter thought he saw a look of vague embarrassment pass across Mather's face. "After seeing the news report last night my memory was jogged and I looked his name up on the computer this morning. I do not know the substance of the matters but as you know, each case file is listed." He had caught him out.

This was a blatant lie and confirmed his suspicions about Hale. Mather would not know how to look up a client. He did not appreciate being spied on and it confirmed the rumour within the building, Big Brother was always watching.

Mather concluded "Peter, if you ever want to join us on the top floor, deal with this case in the appropriate manner." Peter was more determined than ever to scrutinise the files and, acquiescing to all Mather's demands, he quickly made his excuses and headed back to his office.

TEN

Naomi Brahman was a beautiful woman and she knew it. It was not something she felt conceited or bragged about. It was a fact, and in her barrister's gown and wig she turned many heads.

As she read over her counsel's notebooks for cases that day in the crowded smoke-filled barristers' waiting room in the Old Bailey, she felt anything but royal. Truth be told she felt faintly ridiculous, she always did in her grey pinstripe, white blouse, black gown, white collar and grey wig.

She was still angry at the outcome of the R.V Roland case. She finished reading her notes and remembered back to the outcome of the trial, the jury had taken only thirty minutes to make their decision, then she had phoned Peter to give him the bad news. Fiddling in the pockets of her suit through the armholes of her gown, she found a twenty pence piece and, holding it poised above the coin slot, she dialled the number she knew off by heart. "Martin Mather & Co. How can I help you?" Naomi quickly inserted the coin and pressed the answer button. After a delay that ate nearly all her funds the phone was finally picked up, then she waited until eventually a surly receptionist put her through to Peter.

"Naomi darling, do I get bad news or the bad news first, confirm my worst fears." He was always so goddamn cheerful.
"Well, the jury came back in record time. Hodge summed-up in thirty excruciating minutes. No prizes for guessing at whom his ammunition was

aimed? The jury went out at eleven-thirty and came back in at twelve o' clock. Just before lunch, which pleased his honour no end, causing him to thank them for their quick decision and heap praise upon them."

"Oh dear, I'm sorry," Peter mumbled apologetically, interrupting her flow.

"Never mind that Peter, the case was pretty much dead in the water. What I am worried about is the length of time the jury came back in. I mean, in ten years as a barrister I have never had a jury out for less than an hour. I mean my defence did not even leave an inkling of doubt in their minds."

She really was worried. It was a cold world out there for barristers who failed to perform. They were always judged upon the result in their last case. The case of Roland could ruin the career that she had carefully built up over the last ten years. Not to mention the false caring looks of concern that she would earn from certain colleagues from her chambers who would revel in her downfall.

"I take it they found him guilty then?" Peter interrupted again, trying to be humorous.

"Of course they found him guilty, they didn't have much option after Hodge's hatchet job on our defence. Sentence has been put over for a month and the client has been remanded in custody pending the usual reports," Naomi replied harshly.

"I'll see you later shit for brains," Peter had whispered down the phone.

"Love you too," she replied.

Returning to the table and gathering her brief, she headed to the barristers' robing room to change before returning to her chambers in Middle

Temple. She had said "Love you too" so easily. It had rolled off her tongue convincingly enough. But did she really love him? What was she doing going out with Peter? He was not particularly good-looking, his life was a complete mess and he had no money to speak of. He lived with her in her Kensington apartment, got under her feet and had turned what was once a smart bachelorette pad into a hovel. But somehow, despite all his negative traits, she loved him.

That fateful chambers Christmas party they had enjoyed an innocent flirtation that she had no desire to take any further. In fact he flirted with all the female barristers in her chambers. It was seen by all of them as harmless fun. Now it had become something else, something more serious. Something that she did not understand. It scared her and she was not sure that she could cope with it. It had been fun to start with, still was if she was honest. But the nature of the relationship had changed. She could not remember when, but it had taken a turn. Matured into something serious. She did not have time to think about it. She had work to do back at chambers.

Turning down the narrow Old Bailey lane towards Ludgate Hill, she decided to walk the half-mile to her chambers. The fresh air would do her good. She had long ago given up worrying about individual cases. As a pupil she had taken her work home with her. Living out each emotional turmoil as if it were her own. The pressure had been immense. In the end she had to learn to shrug it off. She did not have the time, inclination or energy to become too personally involved. The Roland case was a defeat. But nothing more than a statistic, a blip, a small hiccup in her otherwise blemish-free record. She would redeem herself with a spectacular win in the next case. She smiled to herself. Things had turned out alright in the end. She and Peter had been going out for almost two years and although she found him immensely frustrating at times she was generally extremely happy with the arrangement. Two weeks after that fateful night he had moved into her apartment. It had seemed the right thing to do at the time.

It had started inauspiciously at first. In fact if anything she would not have given their relationship five minutes that first morning.

It had been Christmas 1993 and the whole chambers had assembled for the usual jamboree of free champagne in their cramped basement chambers. They had invited all their current instructing solicitors along with representatives from other firms that they hoped to woo in a drunken moment. Naomi found these affairs tedious and rarely stayed long enough to see the first solicitor pass out from seasonal over-indulgence or, the normally straight-laced, head of chambers wearing a hideous party hat.

It was not that she was a prude, far from it. She had long ago immersed herself in all things British, much to the disgust of her parents, developing a passion for British men of all colours and religions that left a battlefield strewn with the wreckage of many a failed relationship.

Her thoughts reverted to her first meeting with Peter. He had, as he always did, arrived late and drunk. He was celebrating another judicial victory. He was, she thought, a breath of fresh air to the proceedings. They had settled down in one corner of one of the cramped offices and had proceeded to drink as much as they could. They got on famously and she laughed at all of his terrible jokes. The rest was oblivion, although she did recall a stumbled dance with a young barrister in his pupillage at the end of the evening.

The next morning had been a huge shock to her. She woke up at 11.00am, naked in her bed. Facing the bedside table she noticed that her radio alarm clock was flashing the time at her. Her head hurt with the acute pain of her over-indulgence. Opening her eyes to more than a squint caused her temples to pound mercilessly. Looking across the bed to the bathroom door she noticed for the first time the prostrate form of someone else cocooned under the duvet in the bed beside her. His hairy leg poking out of one corner. Quite an attractive leg.

She was not shocked to see someone in her bed, it would not have been the first time. What did worry her was her total lack of recall. If someone ended up sleeping with her she usually orchestrated events and she never had one-night stands purely for the sake of it. She only slept with people she really liked. People who she wanted to go out with. Not that there had been that many. She was not easy but she did not consider herself a vestal virgin either.

A vague puncture of recollection reminded her of the party and the young barrister she danced with. She pulled herself together. What else could she do? Turning quietly to face her conquest she touched him on what she supposed must be his shoulder and shook it vigorously.

The body beneath the duvet gave a low groan of semi-consciousness and turned sleepy-eyed towards her. His face was largely submerged within the protective depths of the quilt. All she could see was the messy brown hair and lightly tanned forehead. Deep within herself she knew who it was but hoped that she was wrong.

She decided to take the bull by the horns and, taking the edge of the duvet whipped it back. Exposing not only her breasts but the upper torso of the man. Her worst fears were confirmed. It was Peter. Looking at his finely chiselled face, aquiline nose, lightly tanned olive skin and mop of thinning brown hair he looked more appealing to her than ever before. His vulnerability as he lay there in his unprotected slumber struck a chord within her. She had not planned this liaison however, and the thought of him waking scared her. What was she going to say? What had she said last night? What had they done? Acute embarrassment at things forgotten, wiped from the minds by alcoholic excesses, swept over her. Threatening to drown her. Put simply, she wanted to die.

Peter opened his brown eyes and smiled at her, intensifying her discomfort. Moving deftly across the small space between them he put his arms around her waist, kissed her lightly on the forehead and snuggled into her side. Shocked by this apparent familiarity between them, all she could do was freeze. If he professed undying love to her she would scream. Commitment, more than anything else, scared her to death.

"Good morning darling. Did you sleep well?" he muffled into her left breast. She knew then that everything was going to be alright. Peter had not professed undying love to her, in fact if anything he had been nonchalant about the whole thing. Over a lazy breakfast at which she said very little he had laid her fears firmly to rest.

"Naomi, what happened last night was wonderful. But I would not want you to get the wrong idea. Just say the word and we can forget all about it." He was a misogynist, a chauvinist but he had said the right thing. He did not want any commitment.

Despite herself she found herself saying: "Well I don't know. Why don't we carry on as we are and see how we go. No commitment. No obligation. No recriminations."

Peter had beamed a masterfully seductive smile at her and replied: "I was hoping that you would say that."

Naomi arrived at the station and looked at the timetable, half an hour until the next train to Guildford, she decided to grab a coffee and magazine while she waited.

ELEVEN

Having returned from his chambers to his mews house, the judge had slept fitfully all night. He had been weak on his journey home. He knew his driver must have noticed it in his face. He had not even gleaned any joy from seeing his beloved car. A beautiful maroon Rolls Royce Silver Cloud which he had bought brand new in 1958. It was still his prized possession but the night before it had offered him no solace.

He had felt cold and clammy despite the fact that the damp grey winter afternoon had been unusually mild for the time of year. He felt in his pockets for his leather gloves. They were not there. In fact he had not seen them for some time. Perspiration had formed in droplets across his forehead and he was forced to daub it delicately with his handkerchief to prevent droplets channelling down the side of his nose and drizzling noiselessly into his lap. His skin felt oily and inhuman to the touch. Nausea gnawed at his guts. He had seemed to stick to the cream leather and it took all his mental will to make it to the car without assistance.

He had not waited to watch the driver put the car away in the integral garage and instead had fled into the relative safety of his home. Locking and bolting the door behind him, he had almost forgotten to deactivate the alarm system in his confused state.

He had only had it installed a few weeks ago after a particularly annoying burglary. They had broken in through the bathroom window at the back. Nothing had been taken as far as the judge could see and the only room they went into was his bedroom. The police said that it had probably been opportunists striking on impulse. He must have disturbed them when he came home. Whoever they were, they had rifled through his wardrobes and drawers and thrown all his clothes into a huge pile in the middle of the room. Putting it down to mindless thugs, he had decided to put in an alarm in case they decided to come back for some of his more valuable furniture downstairs.

The mews house was elegant but small, perfect for the life of a bachelor in London with its two bedrooms and bathrooms, study, kitchen and dining room. He had bought it thirty years ago. Belgravia was the fashionable area it had always been and as such it suited the judge and his grandiose aspirations. It had suited his needs. He was rarely in and either dined out with friends or at his club. On the rare occasion that he did need to cater for himself, his housekeeper, who came in three days a week, would make arrangements.

Standing in the hallway for a few minutes wrapped in his camel hair Crombie coat he pondered the mysterious phone call. He quickly dismissed the option of calling the police. He could not risk public exposure if the blackmailer really did know anything. He called him a blackmailer because he did not know what else to call him. He was not after money but he clearly was after something. What did he have other than money that anyone could possibly want?

The antique grandfather clock in the hallway chimed three o' clock, frightening him nearly out of his skin. Moving to the hall table and shrugging off his coat and hat, neatly placing them on the chair beside the table, his colourless reflection stared back at him from the gilt mirror hanging above the table. He did not know why he bothered with mirrors. He hated the damn things. Especially as he had aged. His eyes were already rimmed with red from the strain he was under.

Reminded of his father as he always was in moments of severe stress he realised that, now more then ever, he was a carbon copy of him the day he died. His father died of a massive heart attack when he was ten years old. The judge smiled at himself as he remembered that day. It was the happiest moment of his life.

He had been sitting on his mother's lap in the morning room. They had been laughing and giggling together when the reverend stormed into the room. His father was clearly in a rage and his face was beetroot red. He was brandishing a crumpled up newspaper in his hands.

"Ruined! We're ruined!" he screamed at the top of his voice.
"What do you mean dear?" Bronwen had fearfully replied.
The judge had begun to shake with anticipatory fear and, wriggling himself free from his mother's lap, he scurried into the nearest corner.
"You did this to me," the reverend screamed. "You will surely burn in hell for this," he continued.

The judge turned himself in to face the corner of the room, waiting for the inevitable to begin, and began humming ring-a-ring-a-roses to himself quietly. He ran his eyes over every detail of the corner of the room. He saw a spider's web in the cornice at the top of the wall. He watched transfixed as a spider moved across its web towards a fly that was trapped in its intricate and deadly latticework. Crossing his arms over his head he shut his hands tightly over his ears to block out all sound. He failed and instead heard every word. Desperate to escape he began to hum louder.

The judge suddenly felt himself wrenched backwards from the corner by two strong arms. He was suddenly staring into the demonic face of his father as he had many times before. He began to shake the judge up and down. He felt his bones jarring inside him and braced himself for the inevitable attack.

"I think you are old enough to feel God's might now you little bastard," spat the reverend. He could smell his father's rank breath on his face. His father's face was twisted into a demonic mask, his eyes rabid and his gums pulled back from his teeth in a satanic snarl. Not the caring kind God-fearing reverend known and loved by the community, but the irrational bully that was his father.

He saw his father pull back one arm, ready to hit him. To hit him like he had hit his mother many times before. He closed his eyes, waiting for the impact. He heard his father take a sharp pained breath. Opening his eyes he saw that his father's face was contorted in pain. His eyes bulging out of their sockets. With a sigh the reverend collapses, taking the judge with him. He landed heavily on top of him, knocking the air out of his lungs.

It was only later that the judge realised that his father had died from a massive heart attack brought on by the shock of losing his modest investments in the depression of 1929. He believed for years that he himself had struck him down. He was glad that he was dead, no one would ever hurt his mother again.

Looking at himself in the mirror he suddenly felt desperately old. His body ached with tiredness. He never regretted his father's death but he often imagined how different it all would have been if he had been the product of a normal happy family. His mother had become the sole focus of his life until she had died in 1960. That had been a sad, bleak day for him.

Turning away from the mirror without looking back he had decided to go straight to his bedroom. He was so weary that he found it difficult to climb the stairs. Reaching his bedroom he had not even bothered to draw the curtains and collapsed on the bed fully clothed. He was asleep within minutes.

He dreamed of Eton. He dreamed of Humphrey. He had met Humphrey some years later at a function. He had several grandchildren and was a retired policeman living in Kingston. For him it had been a passing phase, for the judge it had not been that simple. He dreamed of something long forgotten.

It had been a cold winter morning during his second term. He had gone to Humphrey's study to wake him up. It was still dark. Humphrey had asked to be awoken at 6.00am on the pretext of studying for a test that morning. Dutifully he had entered the stale-smelling study dressed only in his pyjamas and dressing gown at precisely 6.00. He noticed that Humphrey was a foetal lump hidden beneath the bed sheets. He shook the unconscious form in the bed.

"Humphrey. Wake up. It's Hodge. It's six o' clock." Humphrey gave a groan and turned his sleepy face towards him. His hair was sticking up. He smiled. An uneven smile made up of stained teeth that were too small for his mouth. He had a plump face with a hooked nose sticking out in the middle, golden hair and blue eyes. Without his glasses on his eyes had been reduced to a pair of blinking slits. It was not an attractive face and was something akin to that of an elf.

Staring at Justin he smiled again. Twice in one morning, he must be ill. Turning on the light Justin moved to the other side of the compact study and began to make the tea. Once the tea was ready, steaming in the cup, he turned back towards the bed and carried the cup and saucer carefully over to the bedside table. Humphrey had returned to a foetal position. He quietly placed the cup on the bedside table.

"Your tea Humphrey." Humphrey opened his eyes and stared at him again. A peculiar look came into his eyes. His cheeks flushed slightly. "You know Hodge you're not a bad-looking fellow at this time in the morning. Gives a chap something to get up for."
"Thank you Humphrey." He had been

embarrassed.

"Is there anything else Humphrey," he stammered. Still smiling, Humphrey had sat up in the bed energetically. He was not wearing a pyjama top. Taking his tea from the table he drank it quickly with enthusiasm, never taking his eyes off him. Folding back the sheets Humphrey got out of bed and stood beside him. He was naked. He had never seen a naked man before. Something stirred in him at that moment as he flicked his eyes up and down the naked body before him.

It was not that this body was anything remarkable, if anything Humphrey was a little on the short side with skinny, stumpy legs. He was no sportsman and his body had given way to flabbiness. It was simply that he never seen an adult's body. Humphrey's penis was showing the first signs of erection. He made no move to hide it. Justin quickly tore his eyes away and felt his cheeks fill with the warm blood of embarrassment. Looking back, he saw that Humphrey was still making no attempt to cover himself and was still smiling his predatory, crocodilian smile.

"Yes Hodge. My little man I think there is something else you can do for me."
"What?" He had barely been able to get the words out. His throat was dry.
"Get me my dressing gown. I prescribe some vigorous exercise for you this morning and every morning until you are a fit little soldier."

The judge had stumbled his way to the back of the door for the dressing gown where it was always hung on a hook. What was happening to him? What was it that he was feeling? He handed Humphrey his dressing gown. Humphrey slowly put it on and tied it around his waist.

"Shall I put on my games kit, Humphrey?"
"No, Hodge. We're going to take our exercise in the shower block."

The judge had been in and out of a deep sleep ever since he had returned to his house the previous afternoon. It was as if he was in the grip of some massive delirium, he neither knew what time of day it was nor in fact even what the day was. Waking up at some time in the morning still fully clothed on the bed he had managed to drag himself to the phone and call his clerk, saying that he would not be in today, that he had flu. In fact, although he was almost completely unaware of what he was saying, he did not think he was lying.
He had not eaten and had staggered back up to his bedroom where he once again collapsed, returning to the haze of half reality, half fitful imagination that demanded to swallow him up.

Sometime later he was awoken by the sound of the telephone ringing in the downstairs study. Sitting up in the bed he noticed that it was dark. He switched on his bedside lamp. Looking at his watch he saw that it was ten to four in the afternoon. He could hardly believe it. He had slept for at least seven hours. It had certainly done him some good he thought to himself. He almost felt himself again. His body had stopped aching and the sweat had gone. What disturbed him was that neither his housekeeper nor his driver had disturbed him. If they had come in they would have woken him. Perhaps he had phoned them and told them not to but if he was honest he could not remember.

He had not washed or shaved in what seemed like days and he could feel the grime of the fever on his skin. Disgusted with himself he decided to take a bath as soon as he had answered the phone. Swinging his legs off the bed he stood up and his legs fell out from under him as a wave of dizziness swept through him. He almost fell and only saved himself by grabbing onto the chest of drawers by his bed. He loosened his tie and collar button, which appeared to help. He felt short of breath and his chest was tight. He could hear his own deep ragged breaths wheeze in and out. If he did not answer the phone the alarm might be raised. He did not want people snooping into his life or his home for that matter.

After a few minutes he felt much better and braved the stairs, taking each step slowly. As he passed the hall mirror he tried not to notice that he looked very grey and that the effort of movement had soaked the collar of his shirt with sweat. It must be the lack of light in the hall, he thought to himself. He had not bothered to turn on any lights as he went and relied instead on the pool of light flooding from his bedroom to guide him.

Reaching the study and switching on his desk lamp he wondered whom it could be calling him. He did not want to admit it, but the dread in the pit of his stomach suggested that he knew exactly who was at the other end of the line. Thinking about it brought the pain back to his chest in a dull, irritating thump. This time the pain was travelling lightly up and down his right arm, causing it to feel slightly numb. Curling his biceps and clenching his fist he stood over the telephone as it continued to shrill systematically.

Mustering all his courage he picked up the phone and endeavoured to sound normal as he spoke. "Hello. Who is it?" He held his breath for what seemed an eternity as he waited for the inevitable reply on the other end.

Suddenly his answer machine clicked on as he spoke and began to play back his message. He left it on at all times so that he could field all his calls and only talk to people when it was absolutely necessary. He had an irrational fear of phones and he had always done his level best to avoid using them. The message tone sounded down the phone. He heard a mechanical click.

"Good evening Your Honour." The robotic voice grated. "I'm glad you're in. I tried to reach you at your chambers, your clerk said you were at home ill. I trust it is nothing serious."
The judge could not reply. He could not think of anything to say.
"I would like you to do exactly as I say. Do you understand?" The voice continued devoid of any emotion by whatever machinery that was creating it.
"Yes," the judge replied quickly.
"I would like you please to switch on the television. I know you have one in your study."

He had to have been in his house, how else could

he have known what room he was in. What the room contained. He had been in his house, or worse, he was watching him from some vantage point. He was too weak to argue.

The voice continued "Time is very short and if we are to conclude our business there is something I want you to watch. May I also suggest that you pour yourself a drink from the marvellous drinks cabinet? This may be quite stressful for you."

"What channel have you got it on?"

The judge had not even noticed. He looked at the screen. "BBC 1."

"Good. Well I want you to turn up the volume and watch the next item. I think you will find it most interesting."

An item about the death of a London prostitute began to play. He did not recognise the name. "I do not see what this has to do with me whoever you are." The voice did not need to reply. A picture of Bobby appeared on the screen.

Suddenly the judge knew only too well who it was.

"You can't say where you were two nights ago can you, Your Honour? But I know where you were and who you were with last Wednesday, don't I?"

He had been with Bobby last Wednesday. A torrent of pain ripped through his chest before he could say or think anything more.

Lying on the floor face upwards as his vision began to tunnel into a far nirvana he thought, he hoped, that he would die. The alternative was too shocking for him to contemplate. Lying on the floor he began to think about God, he had never been a religious man, his father had put paid to that. He had always been proud to boast that there was no heaven, no God and no Jesus at his right hand. As he blacked out he hoped, he prayed, that he was wrong, that he would be going to a better place.

TWELVE

Peter returned to his office and shut the door quietly behind him. He had been unnerved by his conversation with Mather. He had expected a sound reprimand. Instead he had been given some sort of pep talk.

Mather had given way far too easily on the question of Naomi's future instruction. He was up to something. Maybe he would find out what when Paula brought him Bobby's old case files. What was certain was that Mather had clearly offered him the future prospect of promotion, a dream that he had long ago given up.

Paula brought the relevant files to Peter at four o' clock. Initially he was disappointed to discover that, on the face of it, they did not amount to much. In total there were four dusty thin files. His average case ran to three or four additional files.

Each file was a different colour, one red, one blue, one green and one yellow. Paula being ever orderly had placed them in date order with the oldest on top. There was also a sealed deeds document from the strong room emblazoned with Bobby's name in thick black marker pen on the front.

The first one proved to be the least interesting, as this related to the first time he had met Bobby. The facts of which he was largely familiar with. The blue file was equally uninspiring as it only contained three pieces of paper. A note of a meeting with Bobby to give instructions for a Power of Attorney over his estate in the event that

120

something unfortunate should happen to him.

Bobby had called him out of the blue almost two years after they had met for the first time. Peter had been surprised to hear from him. He had been concerned that if he contracted AIDS he might eventually become unable to look after himself or his affairs. He had said at the time that he had no intention of incurring such retribution for working in the world's oldest profession but he had to guard against the possibility. They had not had the chance to talk much on this occasion as Peter had taken the instructions over the phone. Which was perfectly normal in a simple Power of Attorney. There were no complex specific power clauses to draft. Had it been complicated he would have asked him to come in. On reflection he now wished that he had done just that perhaps then he would not be faced with the myriad of questions before him.

The Power of Attorney was given to one Charles Napier. When asked to explain the nature of their relationship Bobby had explained that they were flatmates and very close friends. Peter had suspected that there was more to it than that but it was not his job to pry into his clients' private lives.

He had discussed the matter with Naomi on various occasions. He had always considered himself to be fairly liberal when it came to homosexuality and prostitution. Some of his best clients were prostitutes, female prostitutes as Naomi had pointed out to him. The thought of having a male one as a client had made him feel slightly uncomfortable and he did not want to inquire too deeply. Naomi had laughed at him when he told her that he considered himself liberal. She said that if he was liberal then there was no hope for humanity. He had countered with the oft-mooted argument that he did not care what people got up to in their private lives as long as they did not ram it down the majority's throat. Naomi was amused thinking that he had no concept of liberation!

She illustrated her point by asking him how many homosexuals he knew personally. He had of course been caught out because as far as he knew he had never met any, let alone known them. He had countered by asking how many she knew. He had been overwhelmed to discover that she knew quite a large number and proceeded to name names, both male and female. Some of these people had been friends or associates of his for a number of years and he was shocked that he had never guessed.

She had shocked him even more when he had asked her if she had considered sleeping with another woman. Instead of giving a definite no, as he would have expected, she had said that in the past she had certainly thought about it. At the end of the conversation he honestly could not, any longer, consider himself a liberal.

The green and yellow files proved to be infinitely more interesting as they had involved more personal contact with Bobby. With the Power of Attorney he had drafted the document in less than half an hour and posted it together with his bill. He did not know if the power was ever affected as it relied upon Bobby swearing the power at any solicitor's office. Since he had never returned the document to him for storage in the strong room he would never know.

The green file contained instructions, draft and copy will. Some six months after he completed the Power of Attorney Bobby had called him again. He wanted a simple will prepared. Peter explained that he did not draft wills anymore but would be happy to pass his instructions on to the relevant department. Bobby had insisted that he draft it himself and had invited him to lunch to discuss the matter and take the instructions. Peter had been reluctant to tread on anyone's toes in the Wills and Probate department, but after getting their initial clearance he had agreed to do it.

He had spent six months in the Wills and Probate department during his two-year training contract and although he was rusty he thought that he could manage a simple will. Bobby assured him that it was simple. Besides, he was intrigued to hear what had happened after their first meeting. Peter had never found out after he had left the police station. He presumed that nothing had ever come of the matter. Two weeks after their discussion Peter had received £200 in cash from Bobby with a cheerful note thanking him for his assistance and saying that he would contact him again if he needed him.

He had not been so sure about the lunch invitation. It was not common practice for him to visit the clients at home unless they were important, or very rich. And as far as he was concerned a common prostitute could not be either. Bobby however had been very persuasive

again and they had set a date for the meeting.
Peter made it quite obvious that he was doing
Bobby a favour.

A week later Peter had travelled to 2 Berners
Street, Soho, London to meet Bobby. On the
journey he had cemented his preconceived ideas
about what Bobby's accommodation would be.
More than likely he would live in some squat with
fellow rent boys. It would be squalid and filthy,
full of spaced-out and drugged-up people.

The address he had been given bewildered him.
Soho was a smart area although certain areas
were still fairly seedy and rundown. He did not
know Soho well, but he had eaten out in
Chinatown on many occasions. In recent years
Soho had been cleaned up. Many of the porn
shops and sex shows had been replaced with
smart boutiques, restaurants and the media
companies that had flooded the area. As far as he
was concerned this was still a front for the more
depraved Soho that he had known as a teenager
with prostitution and drugs lurking behind the
façade. He was sure that this was where Bobby
would live.

Since it was a hot summers day Peter had decided
to take the tube. It was a short walk from Oxford
Circus station down the Tottenham Court Road
and then the fourth road on the left. He had left
slightly earlier than necessary, so he wandered in
and out of the shops along Tottenham Court
Road, enjoying the weather and the bustle of busy
shoppers. Turning into Berners Street he was
stupefied to see that it was a pleasant road lined
with office buildings and the occasional shop. He

did not have to walk far to find number two. Above a modern office building, it was one of six flats. The entrance lobby was at the side of the main entrance to the office. Each tenant had their name written beside the entry phone buzzer.

He pressed the buzzer not sure that he could possibly have the right flat. Even if the name told him otherwise. After a few moments Bobby answered and let him in. The flat, which was on the second floor above Office Angels, was a revelation to him. It was small and modern, nicely decorated. It was not luxurious, but comfortable. He was shocked to realise this was how he would decorate his own home. Instead of tacky furniture, bright colours, pictures, statues of semi-naked men, mirrored ceilings, waterbeds and leopard skin sofas, it was a picture of understated elegance.

The front door opened into the main area of the flat, a large living and dining room with one corner devoted to a small kitchenette of smart white units. Off to the right of the kitchenette was what he presumed were the bedrooms and bathroom. Bobby was dressed neatly in a pair of tight black jeans and an expensive looking white shirt that was open at the neck. The arms of which were neatly folded to just above the elbow, exposing a Tag Heuer watch. His hair had been cut since their first meeting and was fashionably short.

"What did happen after our first meeting?" Peter asked, unable to contain his interest.
"Nothing to explain really Peter. As soon as you left they knew the game was up, I had won. They

didn't like it but they had to let me go. The charge was dropped of course and I wandered out a free man. You should have seen their faces, I tormented them to the point of distraction. They hated the fact that they could not touch me. A few of them were itching to have a go at me."

"What do you mean, beat you up?"

Peter was not so naïve that he believed people held in custody did not occasionally have unfortunate accidents, but he could not believe that they would let a prostitute dictate their behaviour. He knew a few policemen who would not deliberate, they would beat him up and ask questions later. Intimidation was a fact of life no matter how politically correct the police pretended to be.

"Yes that's exactly what I mean. A few of them had to be restrained by the others. I enjoyed it so much, you can't possibly know how much."

Peter could certainly imagine how nice that sort of control would be.

After a cup of steaming hot coffee they got down to business. Charles Napier was to be the sole beneficiary of his will. It was as simple as that and Peter was annoyed that he had been dragged halfway across town. Peter was astonished to hear that Bobby had quite considerable assets. Over half a million pounds worth in total, including the flat that had been given to him.

"I don't wish to sound rude, but how does someone in your position get that sort of money?" Bobby smiled at him. "Peter, you're doing it again. Assuming that prostitution is nothing more than a means of survival. A way to feed, clothe and warm yourself rather than live on the streets."

"Well isn't it?"

Bobby patiently explained "No. I see what I do as a profession. I perform a service just as important as you do. Only I get paid better. In many ways what I do is not dissimilar to a counselling service. A sex counselling service. Many of the people that are my clients are hemmed in by a society claiming to understand them and their sexuality. For years they have been forced to keep their darkest secret for fear of persecution, ruin and in some cases prosecution. Now that they could come out, they can't, they are strangled by the power of their positions, constantly threatened with potential exposure. I am discrete and confidential. They trust in me completely."

Peter could not agree. "You might say that now, but what about when you began. Surely you were forced to sell your body."

Bobby replied calmly "I appreciate that there are those who have no choice. I feel infinitely sorry for them and I don't like seeing young people on the street any more than you do. Everywhere you look in London you see a darker side of life but for me it was a natural progression. I ran away from home at the age of thirteen with two hundred pounds stolen from my mother's purse. That two hundred pounds cushioned me from reality until I had made my choice."

"What do you mean when you say it was a natural progression?"

Bobby continued "Long before I left home I had known I was gay. Within days I was cruising all gay bars and being picked up by an assortment of men. They did not exploit me, in many ways I exploited them. It was me who wanted to experiment, not them. I knew that I was very attractive. After all why should I starve when I had that rare commodity?"

Peter did not doubt that Bobby must have been a very attractive teenager and he shivered at the thought of an angelic child selling his wares. Bobby went on "Once the money I stole had run out it did not take me long to work out that I could earn a living from having sex with strange men. After all I had been doing it and enjoying it without the benefits of payment. Why shouldn't I do it for money? Pleasure and payment all at the same time. I couldn't lose, could I?"

"It couldn't have been as simple as that?" Peter asked. Peter found the thought of taking money for sex totally repugnant to him.

"I would like to give you the politically correct little boy abandoned routine but for me it really was as simple as that and it wasn't long before I built up a small but select clientele. I wouldn't pretend that I did not have any problems. The odd violent customer and kinky demand that I disliked. But I soon learned how to pick the harmless ones. The ones who would look after me. My reputation spread quickly. I began moving in powerful circles. Soon I became part of an elite cartel if you like."

Peter had the image of Bobby's typical client emblazoned across his brain. The perverted old man wearing a seedy dirty mac with greasy dark hair and an evil unsmiling face.

"Don't these perverts disgust you? I mean they must be repellent."

"Who says?" Bobby replied cheerfully. "Most of them, all of them really are very nice people. Most of them are lonely. Unable to form relationships through the normal channels because of who or what they are, they are forced to go underground. For the most part they want companionship with one of their own. To express who they really are. Sex of course plays a big part but I don't usually get to that stage with them until I know them and I don't do kinky stuff."

"I take it that your clients walk in the most powerful sectors of life?" Peter asked.

"That's right Peter, but don't expect me to name names, I will not. But let's put it this way, I have been privy to certain sensitive information in my time, call it pillow talk if you like." Bobby laughed at his own joke and threw his head back as he did so. He had a deep throaty laugh. The sort that you could not help laughing along with. Peter was well and truly hooked on the conversation and wanted to get to know Bobby. He liked him and felt that they were already friends even though this was only the second occasion that they had met in their lives.

They had interrupted their conversation briefly while they had lunch. Bobby had prepared a raw spinach and avocado salad with bacon and a delicious garlic and wine dressing served with crunchy bread and butter. Peter did not generally enjoy salad of any kind but this was delicious. They washed the salad down with a bottle of 1991 Chateau Neuf De Pap which just happened to be Peter's favourite red wine. As they ate they chatted. Talking about nothing in particular. Peter's head was swimming slightly by the time they finished the bottle and he decided to swing the conversation back to more interesting matters. Looking at Bobby he noticed that his cheeks were slightly flushed and his eyelids had drooped slightly. At least if he was going to get drunk he was not doing it alone. Looking at the ashtray he noticed that they had smoked the best part of a packet of cigarettes between them.

"Didn't your parents look for you? I mean at first they must have been frantic, called the police, searched for you."

Bobby chuckled quietly to himself at this question. "My mother was glad to see the back of me. She had six rug rats under her feet all sired by different fathers, and she was in love again. This time with a low life scumbag called Frank who was out to get every penny out of her that he could. He was violent and abusive to all of us but she never saw it, or at least pretended that she didn't. She loved him, she always loved them, and didn't want the fact that she had six children to get in the way. And they had plans, such adventurous plans."

He paused to light another cigarette before continuing "she had sold the house and they both planned to open a bar in Marbella. Frank persuaded her that we didn't need to go with them. They would go ahead and set everything up. She promised to send for us but I knew she wouldn't. He had no intention of living with us. She arranged for all of us to go to expensive boarding schools while they were away. I had no intention of going to school and ran away the night after they flew to Marbella. They might have tried to find me, which I doubt. I'm now a statistic, just one of hundreds, thousands maybe, of people that go missing every year without a trace. And so I came to London with nothing but a few clothes and the £200 I'd stolen from my mother a few nights before she left. The rest as they say is history."

It was at this point that Charles Napier, the heir to Bobby's not inconsiderable estate, made his appearance. Peter had assumed that they were alone in the flat. He had not heard anything and Bobby had never indicated that anyone else was there. He ambled in from what Peter had postulated was the bedroom. In fact behind the door was a short corridor leading to what appeared to be three further rooms. He shut the door behind him.

He glared at Bobby suspiciously as he sauntered sulkily to the kitchenette. Peter thought he was probably a couple of years younger than Bobby with an athletic androgynous slim figure, tousled brown hair and dark eyes. His skin was professionally tanned to a golden brown. He had obviously been asleep, his eyes were half-closed with fatigue and he was wearing a loose-fitting T-shirt and a pair of boxer shorts. He was not even vaguely embarrassed about being seen in his underwear. His face was covered in downy stubble. Keeping his eyes on Bobby and Peter he bent down to the fridge and helped himself to a half-open carton of milk. He drank from it hungrily.

"That," Bobby explained, "is Charlie, my better half." Bobby looked over his shoulder at Charlie and smiled. "Morning, Charlie, how's the head?" Charlie mumbled some form of reply. "He suffers from the most appalling migraines Peter," Bobby helpfully clarified. "I've never had anything worse than a self-induced hangover myself. Until I met him I never knew how bad they were. Sometimes he's knocked out of action for days. He has to lock himself in a darkened room with complete silence and tender loving care. He's tried everything from diet to the best drugs available, nothing seems to work. You always know when they are going to strike, don't you Charlie?"

Charlie did not deign to reply as Bobby continued. "He gets this tingling sensation down one arm that travels up his arm to his head, then his tongue goes numb. His vision blurs and his speech becomes distorted. Then the pain starts. Migraines are one of the least understood forms of illness in my opinion. Isn't that right Charlie?"

Charlie ignored him and carried on drinking the milk with a demented thirst. When he finished he crumpled up the carton and threw it unceremoniously in the bin.
"I didn't think we were expecting company," Charlie commented icily.
Peter felt his cheeks burn with embarrassment. He did not want to be thought of as a date.
"Charlie. Sorry. This is Peter Ritchie, my solicitor, he's here to take instructions for my will. No need to get jealous. Of course I'm leaving everything to you."

Charlie was clearly not impressed by this introduction. Mumbling something under his breath he left the room. Peter could hear the sound of a bath being run somewhere in the flat. "Don't mind him. He's very grumpy when he gets up. I'm sure I mentioned it to him last night, but he's so delirious he's probably forgotten. He's wonderful when you get to know him but he insists on doing the mean and moody James Dean thing. Thinks it's cool."

Peter thought there was something quite touching in the way that he said this. It was obvious that they were having a relationship. Nothing overt had passed between them. He had not felt threatened by any of their behaviour and although he should have felt distinctly uncomfortable - he did not. It was a bit like his relationship with Naomi, comfortable was the only word he could think of.

"Is Charlie a prostitute as well?"
Bobby laughed again loudly
"God no. A tart he may be, but not professionally speaking. He's in marketing. He was a client originally but he never paid for anything, I was taken with him from the first moment I saw him. A bit unprofessional I know, if I was a solicitor I'd have been struck off. Luckily we don't have a union."

"Doesn't he get jealous?" Peter knew that he was prying but he could not help himself.
"I don't bring anyone back here so he never sees me with anyone. Anyway he doesn't have a problem with it. He sees it just as a job, what I get up to doesn't affect our relationship."
"Where do you take them then? Does your pimp organise things?"
Bobby laughed even louder. "I wouldn't exactly call him a pimp, he's more like an agent, he takes his ten per cent cut. His name is Larry, Uncle Larry to his boys. None of us have ever seen him or spoken to him and I doubt he really exists. The system is so simple it's almost too simple. The clients contact Larry anonymously via a post office box, each of them has a code name, by

letter or note. Larry, whoever he is, then writes or rather types a short note to us detailing the time and dates. It's all code of course. This note is then placed on a notice board in a pub in Waterloo behind all the regular posters and other stuff. He has an arrangement with the landlord. I go down there every day to check the board, it is as easy as that. Larry has a number of low-key flats around London where we meet the clients. As I told you last time we met. The police know all about it but are powerless to do anything."

He was wondering what had happened to Charlie when Paula poked her head round the door and startled him back to reality.
"I've been buzzing you for ages Peter. I thought you'd gone to sleep?" Paula quizzed him.
"No I was just reading through these files. You know how I am when I get absorbed in something."
Paula was put out that she had been ignored for no good reason and snapped "Someone's on the phone for you, says it's urgent. I think you'll want to talk to him."
"Who is it?" Peter was captivated.
"It's Sir Justin Hodge. He said it was an emergency."
He could not imagine why the judge would want to phone him, much less speak to him.

He told Paula to put the call through...

THIRTEEN

Naomi arrived at Guildford town centre. Many of her cases had ended up at the Guildford courts and the journey had become second nature.

She and Peter did not have a car. Living in town it wasn't necessary. Town planners had made their jobs easy by sensibly positioning most of the courts within easy walking distance of a mainline station. Guildford was no exception and the court complex was a short stroll from the station. Guildford was an unusual city in her opinion because it was a mix of old and new with a hideous carbuncle of a cathedral which was the only reason Guildford was perceived as a city at all. It was so ugly that it had featured in the film Omen. It did not surprise her that Damien had been terrified when his parents had pulled up to it. She always looked out for it from her vantage point on the train and wondered whose wisdom it had been to build such a cold monolith in such a prominent position.

She was in a good mood, her conversation with Peter before he left had amused her. She had never been bothered by Peter's teasing over her parents, she thought that they were quite amusing herself. Sunday lunch with her parents had become something of a tradition, a tradition that she tried to avoid as much as possible. Her parents' disapproval of Peter was universal and blatant, although they both professed to like the person, it was the principal of living with a white man that they disapproved of.
They lived in hope that she would find a nice Indian man from a good family to settle down

with. They had long ago given up trying to arrange a suitable match for her, instead resorting to inviting eligible bachelors to the house for Sunday lunch in the hope that she would approve of one. She and her father had barely been on speaking terms for years as he tried to enforce his will. In the end although he never gave up hope of conformity, he had realised that he would lose his daughter forever if he persisted. Fortunately, for her, Peter had taken it all in good humour.

As she thought she came upon the courts. The crown, county and magistrates courts were conveniently situated in the same quadrant as the police station with a car park sandwiched in the middle. The crown court being a one-storey inconspicuous modern building sitting in the shadows of a multi-storey car park. The county and magistrates court shared a building on the right-hand side of the crown court. It was a popular misconception of members of the public and television addicts that all courts occupied historic old buildings with lofty ceilings and marble-lined corridors. The reality was often different, most courts occupied sterile modern buildings with modern plastic furniture, grey carpets and all the modern conveniences the twentieth century had to offer. The Guildford courts were no anomaly.

In the magistrates court, having made herself known to the clerk of court two, where she was due to appear, she made her way to barristers robing room to read over her brief.

The clerk had told her that neither the defendant nor his counsel had arrived yet. She was not surprised. The case was listed for three-thirty but both she and the defence knew that in practice they may not get before the bench for hours. There were two cases listed before hers and no one could predict how long they would take. It was normal for the Crown Prosecution Service to instruct the same barrister for similar proceedings taking place in the same court and she wondered why she had not been given briefs for the other three matters. It could have helped to kill time. Time was the enemy as far as any barrister was concerned and she estimated that she had spent at least a third of her professional life whiling away hours of time in some court or another, drinking endless cups of murky tasteless coffee. A barrister's lot was not a glamorous one.

She was preoccupied by Peter and his unease the night before. It worried her that he had taken it so badly. He had vowed that he would do everything that he could for Bobby Black. He had been determined to ascribe him some dignity in death to make up for the lack of the same he had in the method of his death.

He had remained thoughtful for the evening worrying about Bobby Black and trying to work out what his next step should be. It had annoyed her that he was giving so much of himself, of his emotion, to the welfare of a dead man. Of course she said nothing because it was typical of him. It had become another cause for him to fight for.

Her case still had not been called by four and she decided to visit an old friend who worked in the Crown Prosecution office situated in the crown court. It was only a short walk to the crown court but she put on her coat and carried her umbrella. It was getting colder and the sky was grey, the clouds looked heavy with rain. Naomi could not bear the rain.

The friend was Edward Williams, an old barrister friend. They had done their pupillage together years ago. She had not seen him in a couple of months and she needed someone to talk to, to moan at about their chosen profession. Peter was her lover but occasionally she needed a friend and Edward had certainly been that in the past.

Edward had married two months ago and she wanted to catch up on how marital bliss was treating him. Back in the heady days of their youth they had enjoyed a blissfully short but passionate liaison. It had been purely sexual but still, if she was honest, Naomi had been secretly disappointed when he had married. They had always enjoyed a good friendship despite their earlier history together and continued to flirt with each other. She wondered if this would have changed now he had married Mellisa, a legal executive at Masons.

She was hungry and decided that she would offer to take him to the canteen. Not that the canteen, which was small and cramped, was any good. It had a monopoly on both the public and legal profession who had to stay as near to the courts as possible during the lunch recess. Since the nearest pub offering food was a good ten minutes walk away they had little choice. The food was of poor quality and expensive for what it was, but the only alternative was starvation.

Stopping at the reception desk just inside the glass entrance she asked for Edward to be paged on the public address system. The obliging woman did so immediately.

"Would Edward Williams of CPS please come to reception to meet Miss Brahman of counsel."

Naomi waited for a few minutes and then asked her to repeat the message, asking him to meet her in the canteen in ten minutes. It was not unusual for counsel to ignore messages if they were busy or did not want to be found.

The canteen, sandwiched between two courts, was thankfully almost empty. Sitting at a table near the door she waited for Edward. She saw him before he saw her. Dressed in a dark pinstripe double-breasted unbuttoned suit he was the picture of sartorial elegance, his brogues shined, matching his deep, almost coal black eyes.

She felt an irrational pang of jealousy. Marriage clearly suited him. He looked happy. This piqued her. She had half hoped that he would look thin, gaunt and miserable.

Waving at him she caught his attention. His face lit up when he saw her and smiling he rushed over to the table. She got up to meet him. He threw his arms around her and embraced her firmly, kissing her with subtle ardour on her lips. They disengaged and sat down. He sat opposite her. She could at least comfort herself with the knowledge that he could still kiss her, that he still wanted to kiss her in public. His kiss was as good as she remembered it to be.

"Sorry I'm late. Had an important meeting. Naomi, it's great to see you. You're looking gorgeous as always."

"You don't look so bad yourself Ed. Marriage seems to agree with you."

She patted his stomach where the first signs of a paunch were developing, for emphasis.

He laughed raucously. She laughed too. He was always a fun person to be with.

"It certainly does. You know I don't know how I existed before, honestly I don't. I know it's a cliché but I swear to God it's the truth." He was animated.

"I really enjoyed the service and the reception. It was a great day, thanks for inviting Peter and me."

"Christ Naomi, thank you for coming and thanks for the present."

"How is Mellisa?"

She did not really want to know. She had forgotten what they had bought them. Peter had been dispatched to Harvey Nichols to sort it out.

She did not like Mellisa, with two l's. Peter had claimed she was envious, and he was more than likely right. On the face of it there was nothing wrong with Mellisa with two l's. She was attractive, witty and intelligent, a successful career woman with her own money. Naomi could not put her finger on it. The woman made her restless. She tried to sound genuine but did not convince herself.

"I wish you two would get on better. You're my two favourite girls. You've got to give Mellisa a chance. How is Peter, has he managed to make an honest woman of you yet?"

Peter had been unconcerned about their past history and to her annoyance he and Edward had become firm friends. She did not want them to be enemies but she often complained that Peter could have at least offered some protest.

Peter had proposed to her on a number of occasions. She had always turned him down. She was not ready for the commitment of marriage yet, if at all. The fact that she had been with Peter for two years was a minor miracle. Scared of commitment, the very mention of the M word had in the past sent her fleeing for protective cover. Peter had outlived the time span of many previous relationships and lately she had been considering the possibility that she might actually want to spend the rest of her life with him.

"No Ed, he hasn't." She wanted, needed, to change the subject.
"How is work going?" she continued.
Edward's career had accelerated rapidly since he had joined the Crown Prosecution Service and he was now one of their senior prosecutors handling all sorts of exotic cases.

He had asked her to join up with his team more than once. She had always argued that she did not like prosecution work and her best work was of a defence orientation. This was completely untrue. She did not trust herself with him, which was the height of arrogance, since they had been nothing but friends after the break-up of their brief affair. He had never given her any indication that he wanted to rekindle their flame, and she did not want him to do so, not really. She was happy with Peter, she just liked to cling to one fantasy.

"Pretty hectic as always but I wouldn't have it any other way as you well know."

They both laughed.

"How is it going for you?" Edward asked.

"Oh not too bad, the usual hotchpotch of good and bad cases. Nothing major to report."

"Any juicy cases coming up that I should be aware of?"

She was probing. He was always a hive of information.

Edward laughed.

"You know I can't discuss our cases," he said with mock severity.

"Tell you what, if I offer you a cup of coffee and sandwich of your choice would you reconsider?"

"That sounds like bribery."

"Call it what you like. I'm hungry, I'm going to get something for myself, I was just being amicable. No jury would convict me. Anyway, who am I going to tell?"

She smiled and laughed.

"Oh all right, you just bought a senior prosecution barrister, but never let it be said that I'm cheap. I'll have cheese and pickle if they've got it."

"If I can be sure of anything it's the fact that they will only have cheese and pickle and will have enthusiastically titled it a ploughman's lunch."

He laughed heartily.

She went to purchase two cups of coffee and two 'ploughman's lunches'. Shoving his Styrofoam cup of coffee and plastic wrapped sandwich across the table in his general direction she sat back down opposite him.

"So dish the dirt," she continued.
He was not going to get away with it that easily.

He told her about a number of cases that she had already read about. He did not add much that she did not already know. He always had something interesting to tell her and she knew that he was holding back on her.

"Ed," she interrupted him. "You're insulting my intelligence as usual, I know you're not telling me everything and shyness does not become you."
She knew that she had got him because he looked serious for a minute and leaned forward so that he could not be overheard.
"Listen. There is something, but I can't tell you. It's more than my job's worth, this is so explosive well who knows what the repercussions could be... I'd love to tell you but this order came from the director herself." He sounded very serious.

Naomi found herself laughing in spite of his serious tone. He had a tendency to over-dramatise situations.
"Oh Ed, this sounds like some paranoid conspiracy theory, how big can it be, perhaps it would blow the government apart!"
She was only joking but she saw from his reaction that this was not as far-fetched as she imagined.
She was determined to get him to tell her.
"Ed I'm not going to leave you alone until you tell. You know you're dying to tell me, you wouldn't have mentioned it otherwise."

She studied his face. He looked stern as he pondered for a few moments and then his features collapsed in defeat.

"All right, all right," he conceded. "If I tell you, you have to promise not to tell anyone, and I mean anyone, not even Peter."

Crown Prosecution barristers had a habit of over-blowing their own importance, even Edward whom she regarded as a close friend.

"Okay."

She munched on her sandwich and sipped her coffee as he talked.

"What I'm going to tell you is hot off the press so to speak. It should be common knowledge within a few days. I'll take it as read that you, like all dutiful lawyers, have been following the news in the last couple of days." He paused to look around the canteen to make sure no one else was within earshot.

"The first thing we knew about it was when we were consulted by the police yesterday evening. For now we're keeping a lid on it, but my information is that someone will be taken in for questioning by the end of the day. It's not so much the crime that is a delicate matter as the person they intend to detain that will cause all the problems. Certain information has come to their attention from a third party that compromises this person and certainly puts him at the scene of the crime."

So far he had told her nothing out of the ordinary. It was not unusual for the police to contact the CPS about the possibility of a prosecution taking place if the case was borderline. If the CPS advised the police that they had good grounds for a prosecution they would go ahead, if not, they would not proceed or they would wait until the evidence was conclusive enough.

"The police have informed the Home Office due to the nature of this matter, and MI5 may also be involved, that's how far-reaching the implications are," he continued.

She now knew that this made it an important matter of security and she imagined that it must be a political scandal about to erupt and she wondered which Member of Parliament had been caught with his trousers down this time.

"Like the excellent barrister you are Edward you have failed to deliver two important pieces of evidence. Who? And what?" she interrupted.

He thought about her question for a minute.

"The who in question is Sir Justin Hodge, the what is the murder of Bobby Black."

He whispered this so quietly that she thought that she had misheard him. She knew that her mouth had dropped, that she was staring at him in surprise.

"Remember this is strictly entrée nous. If this ever gets to court, which I doubt, it will be the biggest murder trial of the century. I'm going to pitch for the prosecution myself. This could be the most important case in my career," he finished dramatically.

The impact of what he had just told her was beginning to sink in. A member of the High Court was about to be arrested and possibly charged for the murder of a common prostitute who just happened to be an ex-client of her boyfriend. An ex-client that Peter had identified in the morgue the previous evening. Not only that, but the judge in question was one of her oldest adversaries who had demolished her in court yesterday.

Trying to remain unfazed, she made her excuses, saying she had to be in court, promising to call him about dinner in the next few weeks. She ran back to the magistrates court like a woman possessed and made her way to the nearest public phone. She shook as she tried to find change in her pocket and dialled Peter's office. As she was doing so the clerk of the court called her case. The last thing she wanted was to conduct a mode of trial hearing. Replacing the handset she hoped the case would pass quickly, this was important information and she had to get it to Peter.

FOURTEEN

To say that Peter had been stunned by the conversation that followed with the judge would begin to describe the way Peter felt. The judge had sounded distant, out of breath and in some considerable pain when they spoke. Peter had little time to interrogate him. Speaking quietly the judge explained that he suspected that he had suffered a heart attack. He wanted Peter to come to the house immediately in order to tell him something very important.

He would not say what. Peter asked if he had called for an ambulance, to which the judge had replied that he could do it once he arrived. The matter they had to discuss was far more important. The judge had then rung off after giving his address.

Peter did not exactly count the judge as one of his closest friends, in fact if anything he had always regarded their professional relationship as hostile. Why would someone as well connected as the judge want to call him?

The judge had sparred with most of the great legal minds of the century from Lord Denning to the present incumbent of the post of Lord Chancellor, Lord Irvine. Not to mention many of the people who had gone on to become senior partners of most of the top one hundred law firms in London.

Peter was a good lawyer, but he did not delude himself that he was in the same league as any of the luminaries that the judge could call upon day or night. Whatever it was his curiosity was aroused and he could do nothing else but go to the judge's home. Apart from anything else, if the judge had had a massive heart attack he may be dying, and Peter did not want that on his conscience.

Telling Paula that he had to attend an important meeting and that he would not be back he rushed out of the office and hailed a black cab on the Goswell Road. He only had to wait a few seconds.

The whole journey took less than fifteen minutes but Peter sat on the edge of his seat for the duration. If the judge really was lying on the floor of his home after a major coronary, fifteen minutes would be a lifetime. He imagined the judge perishing on the plush carpet of his living room, his secret untold. What could it be? What could be so terrible that meant he had chosen to rely on him?

He buzzed with anticipation, an almost predatorial desire coursing through his body, electrifying his neurones, pushing energy to each and every limb. He was alert, awake, ready for anything. He simply had to know what the judge's secret was.

Looking at his watch before he climbed into the taxi he noted that it was four-thirty. It was dark. It was raining and his Barbour was dripping with cold rainwater even though he had only been waiting a few seconds. His hair was wet and he shivered as he shut the door behind him.
He did not think that the judge would be worrying about the prevailing weather conditions but all the same he wished that he was in a hot, warm

and sunny place as the taxi pulled up to the judge's house.

The judge opened the door slowly. The house was in complete darkness behind him. His face was a sickly pale pallor in the blanched half-light of the dimly lit afternoon.

Peter was shocked by what he saw. The judge had aged by at least twenty years and his shoulders were slumped forward, his normally bronzed skin looked grey and shiny, inhuman, his mouth pulled downwards into a grimace of concentration and obvious pain. A blanket of some sort was draped over his shoulders, drawn tight over his chest like a grandmother's shawl. His clothes were dishevelled and dirty and Peter detected the faint smell of stale body odour emanating from him.

Eventually the judge spoke. His voice was reduced to a painful rasp as it pushed its way over dry chapped lips.

"The look on your face just told me how bad I look. Now come in, I'm feeling very cold."

Whatever it was that he wanted to discuss he was not showing any signs of gratitude or respect and was behaving in his usual bombastic manner.

Peter did not want to argue with him, if he put him under too much pressure he might drop dead in front of him.

Peter quietly followed the judge through the house to the study. The judge sat down heavily in a chair and indicated silently that Peter should do the same. Peter sat opposite him. He decided to speak.

"Your Honour. Look I'm going to speak bluntly

because, quite frankly, I don't think we have much time. You and I have never seen eye to eye and I do not know why you have asked me here, but whatever it is will have to wait. You clearly need urgent medical attention. I'm going to call an ambulance. I won't pretend that I'm not intrigued, but that will have to wait."

Peter stood up from the chair and looked around for the phone. The judge had made no attempt to speak or dissuade him from his course of action.

Spotting the phone on the desk he dialled 999. The judge made no attempt to stop him and sat quietly watching him.

Peter returned to sit opposite the judge who was still regarding him with his cold clinical eyes. Peter felt very uncomfortable, as did anyone who received that stare in a court of law, that alone was enough to wither the most experienced barrister. What made this doubly uncomfortable for Peter was the fact that he was sitting in the judge's own home. They were sharing each other's personal space, removed from the legal context within which he normally operated Peter felt completely out of his depth, naked, unprotected.

"I think if current government statistics are correct we have about ten minutes to discuss the other matter before the ambulance arrives. I agree with you that there has never been any love lost between us, but I am in what can delicately be described as a somewhat awkward situation. Do not feel overly flattered by the fact that I called you. I knew you always use whatever means at your disposal to clear your clients' names."

The judge spoke clearly and precisely but with some effort and he kept taking deep gulps of air. "Am I to understand that you are instructing me as a client?" Peter asked.

The judge managed a subtle pointed smile. "Correct. I do not think we have the time to chat idly so I am going to tell you as much as I can in the time we have," he answered.

He proceeded to tell him about the telephone calls. He denied that he had ever known Bobby Black, maintaining instead that this was some sick attempt to blackmail him. He suspected that if he did not do what the blackmailer told him that he would be set up in connection with the murder. Peter could not believe what he was hearing. This was a huge scandal. Peter could almost imagine the headlines. As far as Peter was concerned everything to do with Bobby's murder was becoming more and more questionable.

The judge finished talking.

"I do not particularly care if you believe me or not. I know that you are the best man for the assignment. I am going to give you my wife's telephone number. I want you to call her as soon as the ambulance arrives and tell her what has happened. Do not however tell her about the blackmailer, merely tell her about the heart attack. My wife is a very sick woman and I do not think her mental fragility would hold up if she was told everything, do you understand?"

"Do you have any idea who it may be? It may seem a stupid question but I think I ought to know if you have any notion, anything at all?" Peter knew that he was not dealing with his average client here, and he felt slightly patronising as he asked the question, but if anyone was going to conceal facts it was the judge.

The judge gave a rasping chuckle.
"I thought of nothing else as I lay on the carpet waiting to die. And do you know what? It was not as hard as you could imagine, despite the pain I was in, I formulated a list of some forty or so candidates. The ones that I could remember, there may be many more. When you have been a barrister and judge for as many years as I have you do not make many friends, especially when you specialised in criminal law. I could have come up with hundreds more and only a few would be prosecuted criminals. The list could be doubled by the enemies I have made within our hallowed profession."

He paused for a moment and Peter thought he saw his eyes soften slightly with some memory or another.
"Do not feel sorry for or pity me. I have after all been the master of my own destiny."

He dictated his wife's number without waiting for Peter to reply. Peter diligently wrote it down on a piece of paper that the judge had thrust at him. He noticed that it was a Guildford number. As he wrote the number down something clicked within his brain. The phone.

He looked up at the judge. All his other standard questions at a preliminary interview were instantly forgotten.
"Do you know if the answer machine was on when you took the call?"

He knew it was a long shot but it could not harm to try.

The judge thought about this for a few seconds. "I always leave the answer machine on. I like to filter all my calls, you never know who is calling you. Half the time they are wasting my time. I let the machine pick up all my calls and then, if I decide I want to speak to whoever it is, I pick up the call."

The judge stopped mid-sentence. He realised what Peter was getting at.

Peter looked up at the judge.

"The play button is flashing has anyone else called today? Or yesterday?"

"To be honest, if anyone did call I would not have heard them, I was completely unconscious for most of the time." the judge replied nervously.

Peter pressed play. The recording device deep within the machine clicked as it rewound the message for replaying. The LED crystal display printed '1 Message' across its tiny screen, and Peter's heart nearly leapt into his throat. There was only one message recorded. That could only mean one thing.

The message began to play and Peter soon understood why the judge had been struck down by a heart attack. On hearing the mechanical voice again the judge took a sharp intake of breath and clutched his chest tightly.

The whole conversation had been recorded in its entirety. It was chilling listening and Peter felt himself shiver involuntarily.

"Well, Your Honour I think that your blackmailer friend has made his first big mistake. There is no way that he can get away with it. We'll just hand this tape over to the police and let them deal with the matter. If he tries to contact you again the police will be ready. I'd almost say this closes the case, wouldn't you?"

The judge looked up at him.
"If only it were that simple. I'm afraid I cannot let you turn that tape over to the police or to anyone for that matter. The contents of that tape are to be kept confidential between us. If I want it used I will tell you."

Peter could not believe what he was hearing. It was not so much the being asked to ignore vital evidence that galled him, he had done so many times when he was relying on the prosecution to find the evidence. This however was entirely different, this could prove a man totally innocent of murder. To produce it at a later date would give rise to all sorts of allegations. The evidence would itself be tainted by the doubt this would cast across it.

"You have got to be joking?"
"I never joke, Mr Ritchie. I do not want any of this ever getting out. If you can stop it without using that then you will. Certain people will still know even if the blackmailer is stopped, I cannot risk that," the judge said matter of factly.
"What if I refuse to take your instructions unless you allow me to turn this information over to the police?"

Peter knew that if the judge was desperate he might agree to his demand. Peter did not trust the judge at all and he could already sense that they were beginning to play an elaborate game of cat and mouse. He was not telling him everything.

"Oh, I have no doubt you will take the case, Mr Ritchie. This is after all potentially the biggest case you have ever undertaken and could be the making of you as a solicitor. Your reputation could precede you. No more small-time criminal cases in the magistrates and crown courts. It would be the Old Bailey all the way for you. If Mather does not offer you a partnership I will be very surprised, alternatively you could name your salary at any of twenty top firms. You need this case as much as I need your expertise. I know you have already decided to act for me."

Peter knew that the judge was right. This was the big one that he had been waiting half his life for. Peter decided not to answer him straight away and getting up from his chair he wandered over to the phone and removed the tape and placed it in his outside left-hand jacket pocket.

"Look, Your Honour. You heard what he said. It is obvious that he has set you up to take the blame for Black's murder. If he has done it properly the police will be making their way here now. It is only a matter of time. Hand it over now and you have some chance. At the very least they will have to investigate the possibility that you are being set up." He was puzzled that Brown had not already arrived.
"I have thought of that. I am willing to take the risk."
"And are you sure that you never knew Black?"
"I have already told you that," the judge snapped sharply.

He spoke too quickly, too sharply, with too much feeling. But now was not the time to press him further. If the judge lived to see another day, he would find out what it was.

Looking at the phone something else bothered him. Something he could not remember for the moment. The doorbell disturbed his line of thought, the phone instantly forgotten. The near spark of realisation extinguished almost as soon as it had occurred to him.
"Forgive me if I ask you to get that. I am feeling particularly off-colour at the moment," the judge whispered.
Peter let the three paramedics in through the door and pointed them in the direction of his new client. Two of them carried a portable gurney between them while the other carried portable emergency equipment.

He watched frustrated as they lifted him and attached him up to a portable heart monitor and oxygen. One of them said that he had suffered a massive coronary and he was lucky to be alive, the judge was stable but that his heart rhythm was very erratic. He injected him with a drug of some kind. As they loaded him into the back of the ambulance the judge indicated for Peter to come over to him.

Pulling the oxygen mask off his face the judge whispered hoarsely to him.
"Take my keys from the hall table and lock up for me. Bring the keys to the hospital later. Do not forget to phone my wife."

With that the doors of the ambulance were shut and it drove off leaving Peter standing alone in the middle of the road. He could hear the siren on the top of the ambulance wailing as it made its way through the swollen, throttled rush hour traffic.

Making his way back into the mews house he shut the door behind him, he had immediately been put into a position of trust by the last person in the world he would have expected it of. The judge had no one else he could trust more than him and he felt for the judge, just as he had felt for Bobby. He hoped that he would never be in that position.

The judge in one way had correctly assessed his character, he wanted this case more than any other. What he had miscalculated was Peter's need to sacrifice everything for the big one, he would not destroy his life for power and position as the judge must have done. His career was important but not that important.

Finding the keys on the hall table he moved quietly around the house checking that everything was secure. Looking around him he noticed how sterile the whole place was, beautifully decorated it seemed devoid of any character or individuality, lacking any signs of a feminine touch or flourish. It was a bachelor's domain, filled with expensive furniture and antiques organised in a masculine haphazard way. For all its opulence Peter could do nothing but feel sorry for its occupant.

How could a High Court judge become embroiled in the murder of a prostitute and why did a blackmailer want to implicate him in the murder without good reason? If he, Peter assumed that the blackmailer was a he, was looking for a payoff there must have been some connection between the judge and Bobby.

Given what he already knew about Bobby it did not take a genius to make more than an educated guess. The judge must have been a client of Bobby's, which would explain his reticence in allowing the tape to fall into the wrong hands. If Peter had made this assumption then others endowed with a lesser metal capacity would reach the same conclusion. Was he protecting his wife? If her mental state was as unstable as the judge had stated, this was probably the most likely explanation but he was also protecting himself.

He was about to leave for the hospital when he heard a car draw up outside the mews house. Opening the door he saw a police car parked in front of the door. Sitting in the front passenger seat was DCI Brown with a driver and two officers in the back.
Brown looked shocked and angry to see him. Peter had hoped that he would not have to meet DCI Brown for a very long time. He knew that he would have some explaining to do.

FIFTEEN

Lying in the back of the ambulance Sir Justin Gordon Hodge watched the ceiling as it negotiated its way through the traffic. Two paramedics fussed about him checking his vital signs constantly. He concentrated on the sound of his breathing through the oxygen mask. The condensation from his breath misting up the clear plastic.

He had called Peter Ritchie because he was the only person who could deal with the situation adequately. Whether they liked each other or not did not come into it. Ritchie was no fool and he would want to know everything in due course and he supposed he would have to tell him. Where would he begin, how would he find the words? He was frightened, he was now facing the one thing that he had always feared throughout his life, exposure. Exposure of the fraud of a life that he had been leading. If he had been discovered years ago he perhaps could have lived with it, he would have had no choice.

Revealing everything meant delving deep into his own soul confessing all the hurt, the pain, the raw nerves that he had long ago buried deep within him. Somehow laying open his soul to a stranger, someone he neither particularly admired nor respected seemed easier to him. Why did it have to threaten him now that he was nearing the end of his life and career?

The drugs that the paramedics had given him caused him to drift in and out of a state of cognisance. He remembered many of the things that he had long ago forgotten. His mind fixed on one particular incident when he had been at Cambridge many years ago.

It was 1938, his first year reading law. He had been eighteen years old and had thrown himself with gusto into both his studying and socialising. He had made friends quickly within the secretive and exclusive homosexuals rife within the intellectual boundaries of the university. In those days the intelligentsia had considered it bohemian and audacious.

He was sharing a study with a young man of his age named George Bowers, the son of a millionaire industrialist and philanthropist. He had liked George immediately, he was everything that he was not. He was outgoing and gregarious with a huge group of friends, all of whom moved in the right circles. He was handsome and dressed in all the latest fashions, and above all else he was rich, able to indulge almost every whim he desired. George liked to take people under his wing and within a few days they had become firm friends.

He and George went everywhere together. They wined, dined and partied the first year of their studies away. They even took holidays together and the vicious gossips in the college would have it that there was more to their friendship than natural brotherly feeling. Both their sexual appetites were well known within the college, and this was something else they shared. There never was anything more than friendship between them and the judge had often looked upon that year as the happiest in his life.

George seemed to be totally at peace with his nature and came perilously close to flaunting it outrageously on numerous occasions. The judge often had to extricate him from delicate situations by means of bribery. He himself was not so comfortable with his desires and had created a façade that to the outside world appeared entirely normal. He even had a number of girlfriends with whom he could be seen at the various social functions they were called upon to attend. Catering for their sexual needs he and George often frequented some of the less well-known bars and pubs that surrounded Cambridge where they could, for a price, gain anonymity and satisfaction.

It was in just such a place that the judge's world came perilously close to falling apart for the first time. The judge had thanked his luck many times that he had not gone to the pub with George on that fateful night.
George had gone alone and had propositioned an undercover policeman. He was arrested and charged. The judge was not even aware of what had happened until one of his friends came and woke him up in the middle of the night. He had been out of his mind with fear for the next few days as they questioned George, not for George but for himself. What would he tell the police, would he implicate him in any way?

Homosexuality was the severest of crimes and George faced the possibility of an extremely long prison sentence. The judge loved his friend dearly but he would not risk being sent to prison.
That was why, when George sent word that he wanted to see him, he had refused to go. That was

why he refused to give evidence on his friend's behalf when the trial began. That was why none of George's friends gave evidence for him. George would understand. They had talked many times about what they would do if the worst happened. Neither would help the other. They could not risk it. George would understand. That was what the judge had told himself many times over the years. He never found out what George thought.

The trial itself became a media spectacle, one of the most sensational scandals of the decade. The judge like everyone else was forced to keep quiet, he could not even talk to his own friends, for fear that they might expose him. Being a homosexual was enough for the authorities and the judge was amazed at the hypocrisy of the powerbrokers who secretly harboured more homosexuals than any other sector of society. It seemed to him that they were protecting themselves by reflecting the blame onto others.

The judge cried often, quietly in the privacy of his own rooms for the friend he had lost, and vowed that he would never allow himself to be in the position that George had found himself. George had killed himself in prison a few weeks after his sentence, unable to cope with the shame he had brought upon his family and himself.

No one would ever get that close to the judge again. He would control his life rigidly, drive his desires underground where no one would ever find them. For most of his life he had succeeded in doing that. Until he met Bobby when the fantasies of a weary old man overcame restraint. He had found another friend in Bobby, and he had been lost too.

He thought of Bobby. He struggled to control his soporific mind as the medication seized control of him. He had seen Bobby on Wednesday night. He knew that. But there was something wrong. He could not work it out. When he had left Bobby had been alive and well. Had the blackmailer been waiting for him to leave, so that he could slip into the room and kill Bobby?

The judge opened his eyes in the back of the ambulance, he stared again at the ceiling, secured onto the gurney, surrounded by all the paraphernalia, drips and tubes, he watched the ceiling move from side to side as the ambulance negotiated the traffic, his emotions overcame him, tears welling in his eyes. The siren wailing on the roof of the ambulance could have been his grief, if only he could cry that loudly he would. Instead his cries were muffled by the oxygen mask lashed tightly to his face.

SIXTEEN

The mode of trial hearing had not gone well. Naomi had done similar hearings hundreds of times and could recite the procedure in her sleep. That was when she had a clear head, with what Edward told her festering in her brain she had difficulty concentrating at all.

On the face of it the case should have been a simple matter. The defendant had committed a breach of trust, was a person in substantial authority or high degree of trust, and the crime was committed in a sophisticated manner and involved the theft of property of a high value.

After the reading of the charge to the defendant by the magistrates' clerk and once the magistrates were satisfied that the defendant had been informed of his various rights, the prosecution and defence had the opportunity to make their representations to the bench as to the mode of trial. Distracted as she was her arguments were weak and lacklustre compared to those of the defence, she did not give enough weight to the relevant features, and did not counter the defence's arguments for summary proceedings sufficiently.

The bench decided that summary proceedings were the best option and moved swiftly on to the consideration of bail once they had fully explained their decision to the defendant, who seemed overjoyed. Naomi realised that despite the best efforts of the defence team he had no idea what had just taken place. Only criminals who had extensive knowledge of the criminal law began to grasp what was happening.

Naomi had on more than one occasion had to explain to a client that this was not an acquittal, merely a procedural hearing, and not the trial proper. More than one client had been devastated by the news, believing that they had just been found not guilty.

Since the offence was clearly punishable with imprisonment, it was up to her to persuade the court that bail should not be granted. Since the defendant was a first-time offender this would not be easy. In the end after lengthy argument between counsel she managed to convince the bench. This was a minor victory for Naomi and she had at least made up for the poor efforts in connection with the mode of trial.

It was gone four by the time the hearing was finished and she managed to make her way to a payphone. After having exchanged a few pleasantries with the defence team she called Peter's office only to discover that he had left some time ago, had not said where he was going only that he would not be back at the office. She tried his pager, but for some reason he was either not paying any attention to it, which was not abnormal, or he had switched it off.

Mulling over her options she decided that she might as well head home. All she could do was sit around, bursting to tell him as soon as he walked through the door. She would probably start a row, because the frustration of bottling up what she knew would begin to boil over. She knew her temper was legendary, that she could spark off at a moment's notice. Whatever the reason for their arguments they were usually one-sided and never lasted for long. Peter, who never took them terribly seriously, would make some funny comment that would reduce them both to a hysterical heap on the floor. She would go home, pour herself a drink and wait for him to come home. Changing quickly and chucking her files, robes, wig and brief into her carpetbag she left. The days had been subtly drawing in and it was beginning to darken as she walked out of the court building. The fluorescent lights from reception were spread and pooling about her feet into the murky darkness.

It had at least stopped raining, and doing the buttons up on her overcoat to shield her from the chill she headed towards the station, her carpetbag hanging heavily in her right hand.

Stepping down the steps into the dim afternoon light, she realised that she was totally alone as she left the building. Everyone else had either left or were still in the courts battling it out. Delving to the bottom of her bag she found her rape alarm, an innocuous-looking cylinder of metal with a button on top. Having prosecuted many rape cases in the past, she had decided to learn by example. She was not going to be another statistic, another victim. This always comforted her when she was worried and, briefly squeezing it in her hand, she placed it in one of her coat pockets where she could get it if she needed it.

Picking up her bag she headed towards a white van, diagonally across the car park. She knew a cunning little shortcut through the multi-storey car park that cut at least two minutes of the walk.

SEVENTEEN

Since his chat with Peter, Martin Mather had spent the rest of the day patting himself on the back in a smug, self-gratified way. He had, as always, handled the matter with tact and charm. Ritchie was now back in line, he had no doubt about that.

With the Ritchie problem out of the way the rest of the day had run smoothly and with precision. He had spoken to Jenkins about the Randal case. He had told him he was to tread carefully and to inform him if Ritchie attempted to interfere in any way. He made it clear to Jenkins that if he handled it properly he would be considered for a seat on the top floor. What he did not tell him was that a seat would not become available for at least five years since none of the senior partners had any intention of retiring before then. Jenkins had instantly become more amenable to his suggestion.

It was just after four o' clock that the phone call came. He had told Mrs Dailey that he wanted no more phone calls, a command that she normally obeyed religiously.
"What?" he snapped at Mrs Dailey.
"I know you said you didn't want to be disturbed sir, but I think you will want to take this call....."
Mrs Dailey attempted to defend herself against her insubordination.
"I said no calls. I meant no calls. Now leave me alone," he returned angrily.

He had been checking the prices of his Hanson Trust Plc shares at the time and had been distressed to see that they were down two pence yesterday. Thousands of pounds had been wiped off his holding.

"Sir. It's the Under Secretary at the Home Office. He asked to speak to you specifically. He says his name is Booth."

This stopped Mather in his tracks. Trawling through his mind for faces of the party hierarchy that he had met over the years, he could not remember anyone called Booth at the Home Office. His chest still swelled with pride that anyone from the government, even a faceless nobody he had never heard of, would want to speak to him.

Unknown he may be to Mather, but that did not mean that he was unimportant, the corridors of Whitehall were awash with such people. This man answered only to Home Secretary himself.

His first thought was if it could have something to do with the New Year's Honours List. He had always hankered after an honour and wanted to be knighted more than anything in his life. It would be the pinnacle of his distinguished career.

He had been active in local politics, putting himself at the disposal of his local Member of Parliament day or night. He was also a member of his local Round Table and Conservative club where he devoted his time to charitable causes. He did none of this for the sake of the charities but to heighten his profile with the powers that be. He wondered if, at last, he was being recognised for his anonymous donations to the party.

"Why didn't you say so Mrs Dailey? Put him through immediately."

"Mr Booth, what can I do for you sir?" he continued.

Mather tried not to sound too excited.

"I'll get straight to the point, Mather. I don't have much time."

Booth spoke with the clipped tones of a civil servant veteran. Clear, crisp and condescending. He had no time for pleasantries and Mather thought he must be some power-crazed young upstart.

"A matter of the gravest importance has come to the Home Secretary's attention today. Not to put too fine a point on it, this threatens the very stability of the government itself. We know that you are someone sympathetic to this government, and frankly you are in a unique position to help."

Booth paused.

He continued "I don't need to tell you this is all of the strictest confidence. This line is safe, however it would be unwise of you to talk about this on the telephone again. If we wish to talk to you again I will contact you directly. I can assure you that your assistance will not go unrewarded."

Mather was speechless. Did he say that the line was safe, that could only mean that his telephones were tapped. What the hell would they want to bug his phones for? But it was the word reward that really caught his attention, it hung in the air like a golden orb. He knew of only one reward that he desperately wanted.

"Believe me, Minister. I am at your disposal, I will be of any assistance that I can."

EIGHTEEN

"Good afternoon, Mr Ritchie."
DCI Brown stepped out of the car without the vaguest of humour. At least their loathing for each other was mutual Peter thought, detecting a glint of sadism in Brown's hard grey eyes. He felt sorry for any criminal that had to face this man.
"I have to say you were the last person I expected to find here," Brown continued, his voice full of suspicion.
"I didn't expect to see you either, Inspector. I'm afraid I have a habit of turning up when anyone least expects it." Peter replied barely concealing his contempt for the man.

There was one reason that the Inspector would be visiting the judge and he would not be happy when he heard of Peter's involvement. Rejecting a blunt statement of explanation he decided to allow the Inspector to take the lead.
"Is his honour in? I have an important matter to discuss with him."

Instead of replying Peter decided to lock the door and place the keys in his coat pocket. The same pocket that held the answer machine tape.
"I'm afraid my client's not here at the moment."
He paused and looked at his watch for effect and continued.
"In fact he should be arriving at St Bartholomew's Hospital about now. Having suffered a major heart attack I don't think he will be able to discuss anything with you for some time. I am going to the hospital now to see how he is doing. Is there a message I can give him?"

DCI Brown looked as though he was about to lose his temper as he realised what Peter was saying. "Since when has his Honour been a client of yours, Mr Ritchie?" Brown asked barely concealing his anger.

"Since half an hour or so ago. I really do not think I can allow you to talk to him at the moment, I'm not sure the hospital will either. If however you would like to have a discussion off the record I would consider anything you would have to say to my client with the utmost seriousness."

Peter could not help playing with Brown, it made him feel better about the way he had handled the identification at the morgue.

"I don't think you realise the position your client is in. We are talking about serious criminal behaviour, it is imperative that I talk to him as soon as possible in order to eliminate him from our enquiries."

Peter knew what this really meant. If anyone was helping the police with their enquiries, they were being held at the police station until either they could be forced to confess their alleged crime or enough evidence was discovered to charge them. Peter knew the reality. Not many people helped willingly, it was put to them that either they volunteered their assistance or they would be arrested.

"I am sorry, Inspector, but it is out of my hands. My client gave me strict instructions that he was not going to answer any questions. Once he recovers sufficiently, if he recovers sufficiently, I am sure that he will be more than happy to assist with your enquiries. May I ask what you wish to question him about? Or do you intend arresting him at the hospital?"

"I don't think we should discuss it further on the street. Get in the car and we'll give you a lift to the hospital," Brown said reluctantly. The thought of travelling to the hospital in a squad car pleased Peter.

Brown moved to the other side of the car and opened the back door for Peter.

"Thank you," Peer said as he stepped into the squad car. The Inspector slammed the door closed behind him. Peter knew that the Inspector hated being polite to him but he knew that he had little choice.

Waiting until the Inspector sat down beside him they continued their conversation as the squad car made its way out into the rush hour traffic. The two officers remained silent like sentries in the front of the car, their eyes firmly to the front.

Peter decided to play his ace. The Inspector could not possibly suspect that he knew what this was about.

"I take it this has something to do with the murder of Bobby Black?" Peter asked innocently. Watching for Brown's reaction. He was clearly surprised that Peter knew anything but he hid it well. Only Peter with his seasoned eye for the acting prowess of senior policemen could have spotted it.

Brown turned to face him.

"I do not know what your client has told you, of course I would not ask you to contravene your confidential relationship but I must tell you that any information that would clear this up quickly before it blows up in anyone's face would be gratefully received. I am as keen as you are to vindicate the judge which is why it is essential that we have a frank and open interview with as soon as humanly possible."

"Until I am acquainted with all the facts, I am afraid that I could not advise my client to speak openly. Any interview with you, assuming that he is capable of taking part in one, would have to be conducted on a no comment basis. Even if I advised the judge to do otherwise, I doubt that he would."

Peter knew that this would infuriate the Inspector. There is nothing that a policeman hates more than a no comment interview. It is a waste of their time. Unlike with anything else said they cannot infer anything from silence. They are forced to pursue a conviction based on evidence alone. If they do not have that evidence they cannot charge a person, whether they are sure of guilt or not. To prejudice your client in a statement before you knew all the evidence was sheer lunacy. This was what Peter enjoyed about the law, the games he had to play, the strategies he had to deploy. Similarly he knew that Brown could not reveal all his evidence unless it was particularly strong. He almost knew what Brown was going to say before he said it.

"I can't divulge all the evidence. All I will say is that there is solid material evidence which was found at the scene suggesting that his Honour was there. We are also pursuing a lead with a potential witness that has come forward with vital evidence pertaining to the crime."

Peter's mind was racing. Decoding what Brown had said, the police had nothing more than some personal effects and a witness. If they were pursuing a potential witness they clearly had not found him yet. The witness had not come forward but had telephoned anonymously. They could not find him and therefore his statements would be inadmissible in a court of law. If they did not know who he was, they could not serve a witness summons on him compelling him to appear to give evidence.

Unless the material evidence was good he did not think they had much to go on. He was not going to change his position unless Brown gave him something more important than that. The material evidence may prove that the judge was a client, but could it prove that he killed Bobby? At the moment they could only suggest an old man took solace with a homosexual prostitute.

Potentially damaging though it was to the judge's career it did not mean he was a murderer. Brown had clearly pinned his hopes on a confession from the judge.
"You'll have to do better than that if you want me to change my position. Off the record my client may have consorted with prostitutes, which I would deny unless you have proof otherwise, but that does not make him a killer and you know how the case law stands on anonymous witness statements. Especially if they can't be found."

Peter was sure that the judge had not told him everything, but he was sure that he was not guilty of Bobby's murder. If anything this new involvement with Bobby's murder made him twice as determined to discover the truth.

"Hindering the investigation at this juncture will do nothing to further your client's case Mr Ritchie. What I can tell you is that at the moment we are not looking for anyone else."
"Then I don't think we have anything else to discuss until I have had the chance to speak to my client in greater detail."

Peter concluded the conversation. There was nothing more to be gained by talking around the subject. He did however want to discuss something else, something that had been harassing him since he had identified Bobby's body at the morgue.
"Tell me something. Why did you say that I was the only one who could have identified his body? Where was Charles Napier when he was found?"

If the Inspector knew about Charlie then surely he would be the number one suspect. If he was not a suspect then maybe he was the mysterious witness that Brown was talking about. The germ of a defence was beginning to form. If he could pin the murder on Charles Napier he might be able to clear the judge. After all, a court loved nothing better than a story of a spurned lover. A lover so out of his mind with jealousy that he would commit murder. The problem was he knew nothing about Charles or his relationship with Bobby other than what he had experienced briefly at their last meeting. Still Peter had a starting point, once he began digging he might find what he was looking for. Brown looked at him blankly.

"Charles who?"

"Charles Napier. He was Bobby's live-in lover last time I met him. Surely he could have identified the body?"

"We questioned everyone else in the building. They mentioned Black had been living with another man until about a year ago. They didn't know his name, apparently they kept themselves to themselves. Anyway whoever he was he moved out about a year ago. Black lived alone after that and we found no signs of cohabitation at the flat. Whoever this Charles Napier was he seems to have disappeared."

Brown paused as if he knew what Peter was suggesting.

"All of our enquiries on that lead have drawn a blank."

Peter felt sure that wherever Charles was he knew something about Bobby and he was determined to find him.

NINETEEN

Martin Mather could not believe what he was being told by Booth. He had quickly outlined the details of Bobby Black's murder and the alleged connection with Sir Justin Gordon Hodge. What shocked him was the fact that he had lunch with the judge the previous Wednesday. They were not friends, but as members of the Royal Automobile Club in Pall Mall they had fleeting conversations and occasionally lunched alone or with other colleagues.

"The problem is that we do not know how long we can keep his identity from the press. We are exerting all the pressure we can to keep the lid on this one but with something this explosive we do not think we can do so for much longer," Booth continued.

"In the circumstances he will be questioned at the hospital. It is our understanding that Peter Ritchie has been retained by his Honour in connection with this matter. Can Ritchie be relied upon to co-operate with us fully? If he cannot we will rely on you to import the seriousness of the matter to him in the firmest of terms." Booth paused, waiting for Mather's reply.

"Ritchie will do as he is told, Minister."

This was all he could say. If Ritchie would not toe the line Mather would deal with him appropriately.

"The case may contain information of an extremely delicate nature. A solicitor that handled such information with due prudence would earn the thanks of Her Majesty's government. If such information were to get into the wrong hands or become public knowledge the consequences could be grave. If Ritchie cannot handle the case in the required way he would have to be removed. The stakes here are extremely high. Do we understand each other absolutely clearly?"

For Mather it was as clear as crystal. The judge was to be a scapegoat for a potentially massive scandal. Ritchie was to suppress any information that could facilitate the scandal even if this was to the detriment of the judge's defence. This did not bother Mather in the slightest. He had participated in the fixing of cases before, wittingly or unwittingly, and he had been happy to do so. Winning was all that mattered to him.

It was Ritchie that would have to worry if anything went wrong and he did not like to think what exact meaning Booth was giving to the word removed. Booth had told him that he would be in contact in due course and would not give him a contact number when pushed for one. Mather smiled at Booth's reply. Booth was also covering his back. If the shit hit the fan Mather would have no way of proving his connection with him.

He remembered the lunch on the previous Wednesday. It had been nothing special, he had taken a taxi to the club to lunch alone as he did a couple of days a week. He often took refuge in the library after a hearty lunch to have a quiet brandy. An all-male preserve, he knew that he could wrap himself in the years of tradition in a hushed monastic silence.
He loved all the petty rules and regulations, the strict dress code, the exclusive and dear membership fees that ensured that he would only mix with the right sort of people. He also liked the

unpretentious and hearty, if expensive, food they served in the wood-panelled dining rooms.

He had joined the judge for lunch at his request. He had said that he had wanted to discuss the Randal case that he was hearing. Mather had been only too pleased to accept, especially as this would mean that the judge would have to pay.

It was an unwritten rule that if you asked another member to join you for lunch you were responsible for settling the bill. As a three-course meal for two could cost more than one hundred pounds it was one reason why he rarely asked anyone to join him, preferring to lunch alone if no offers were forthcoming.

He remembered exactly what he had eaten for lunch, since he nearly always had the same. He started with the Pate de Foie Gras and melba toast, followed by Dover sole and Vegetables de Jour and a superb lemon syllabub for pudding.

They washed this down with a bottle of chilled Chablis at the judge's insistence. He could not remember exactly what the judge had eaten. They had forgone the coffee and each had a large brandy and a huge Havana cigar. Mather did not smoke but could not help champing on a huge cigar when the opportunity arose. It was a status symbol that he could not resist.
Conversation over lunch had drifted from the Randal case to politics in general, all the subjects he would have expected to discuss with someone who was no more than an acquaintance.

The judge had seemed calm, relaxed, and distant

as he always was when they met. Nothing had been out of the ordinary. While they were enjoying their cigars one of the waiters had approached the table discreetly from nowhere and bending down to the judge had whispered something in his ear. Mather remembered that the waiter was holding a silver letter tray in his gloved hand. On the tray was a plain white envelope with the judge's name printed on the front. The judge had thanked the waiter by his first name and taken the envelope from the tray.

"Sorry, Martin, I'll be with you in a minute," the judge had said. He opened the envelope and pulled out a short note typed on a single sheet of paper. He had held it close to his chest so that Mather could not see what was written on it. It had only taken him a couple of moments to read it, he had then folded the note and placed it in his pocket. Mather could not have been sure, but he could have sworn that whatever the note had said, the judge had perceivably cheered up. He had smiled smugly as if he knew something that no one else in the room knew.

"Problems, Justin?"
He could not help asking. It could be something important.
The judge had laughed. And extending his arm he had patted Mather's hand.
"Affairs of the heart, dear boy, affairs of the heart."

Mather had been shocked by this show of affection between them, especially as there was no real warmth between them. He had not known what the judge had been talking about but now he suspected that he must have been arranging an assignation with Bobby Black.

He felt disgusted at the thought, as a devout Catholic he believed that such depraved behaviour was unnatural and ungodly. More to the point he would have to play down his association with the man. He had a habit of name dropping at every appropriate moment and did not doubt that he had mentioned his 'friendship' with the judge more than once. He would have to distance himself from this, and if anyone asked him he would say that he did not know the man.

TWENTY

Heading across the car park, with only the sound of her shoes on the tarmac for company, Naomi began to feel increasingly uneasy. Looking back again at the brightly lit court building she knew she was being ridiculous and reminded herself no one would be so stupid as to attack her outside a court of law.

A chilly wind was picking up and she pulled her coat collar up around her neck with her free hand. The last thing she need right now was a cold.

Her feet ached, as they always did after a hard day and she dreamed of a hot bath full of Badedas bubbles and a glass of wine.

Her paranoia grew greater still. She was imagining all sorts of things and thought she could see movement in the back of the van. She knew she was being ridiculous but once fear had taken grasp of the senses there was little anyone could do to restore normality. It was like waking up after a particularly frightening nightmare covered in perspiration, clinging to the sheets with an irrational dread that she was not alone, completely implausible but nonetheless real. Never one to bow to adversity she determined to carry on walking.

Gritting her teeth she walked around the back of a grotty van, keeping a wary eye on the double doors as she passed them. It was quite obvious there was no one in the van. The still dark interior told her that much. She almost felt like laughing at her own stupidity and reminded herself again that no one with half a brain would attack someone outside a court of law.

As she stepped around the corner of the van she heard a sound behind her, she was not sure what it was but in her mind's eye pictured the doors of the van opening. She knew she was being idiotic, but she began to walk faster anyway just as a precaution. She decided not to look behind her, there was nothing there anyway.

Suddenly she wished she had looked. A gloved hand roughly grabbed her around the head, covering her face with some sort of cotton wadding. She felt her eyes bulge in their sockets, her head pounding with a rapid rush of blood and adrenaline to her brain. She screamed with terror, knowing that her foe's hand would muffle her attempts to be heard. She always had imagined that she would not be the helpless victim, she would fight, she would free herself. Now she realised how stupid she had been to believe that, the terror that she felt coursing through her veins could never be imagined and she struggled to free her brain from the mind-numbing fog of debilitating alarm that was settling in.

Dropping her bag to the tarmac she tried to free his hand from her face, clawing at them desperately. She could not move her head, she could not see who it was, all she could see was the gloved hand clamped tightly over her mouth. Surely someone must have seen them she thought. Then she realised that she was on the blind side of the van, no one could see her unless they were on the same side. With sinking dread she knew that she had walked into a trap. She cursed herself, she had broken all the rules in the book.

She felt him kick her legs away from underneath her and had no choice but to fall deeper into his vice-like grip. He began to drag her back towards the open door of the van. Desperately she kicked her shoes at the ground. Screaming loudly into the cotton wadding and glove. She bit into the hand with all the strength she could muster, only to discover that her mouth was filling with the cotton wadding.

It was then that she smelt it. It invaded her lungs and mouth, a smell she should know, but what was it? It reminded her of experiments she had done in her biology classes when she was at school. It caused her eyes to water, nausea swamped her. As he dragged her to the back of the van she realised what it was, chloroform.

Her biology teacher had used it to kill rats before they dissected them. If she was going to die, she hoped that it would be quick, painless, like the laboratory rats. Recent cases flashed through her mind and if she had not already been so petrified she would have shook with dread.

This was no ordinary attack, he meant to take her somewhere, this had been planned. Oblivion began to pull her downwards towards a blissful nirvana where she could imagine that this was all a dream. She looked to her left towards the court building. She could not see it. She was about to become a statistic.

As she blanked out all she could think was what a stupid bitch she had been, and how Peter and her parents would be devastated by her disappearance. Her last thought was dim and vague, the rape alarm, she had not even remembered that she had one in her pocket.

TWENTY-ONE

At St Bartholomew's Hospital things had gone much as Peter had expected. Despite Peter's protestations DCI Brown had tried to intimidate the staff into allowing him to speak to the judge. They of course had refused, they would all have to wait until he was out of danger.

Rankled Brown had immediately moved the goal posts by demanding that the judge's house be opened for a thorough search by his men. If he could not speak to the judge he would go for the next best thing. The murder weapon.

Peter knew he could not easily refuse but he had no intention of making it easy for him. Since the judge had not been arrested Brown did not have the inherent power to search the judge's home. Brown would have to make an application to the magistrates court for a warrant. This would take time. The only other method open to him was to persuade the judge to agree to a search. The judge was in no fit state to give any authority and Peter had no intention of agreeing to one on his behalf. Not yet anyway.

"If my client does co-operate with a search I would want this to be made clear in any statements by yourself or your officers."
"That would be implied by the fact that he agreed. After all your client, if he has nothing to hide, has everything to gain and nothing to lose," Brown replied.
"We could only agree, if you give me some idea of what you are looking for and don't tell me that you are looking for a murder weapon as it is my

understanding that Bobby was strangled."

As he looked at Brown's face he could not resist a smile to himself, he had trumped him again.
"You seem to be remarkably well informed about the case, Mr Ritchie."
"I pride myself on my connections."
"Perhaps you would like to share the identity of this particular connection with me? I would certainly like to speak to whoever they are about this infringement of security."

Brown was probing. He could not possibly know about Bowers and he had no intention of enlightening him. No matter what assurances he received he knew that Bowers would be sacked if he revealed his identity.
"You know that I can not and would not do that. It would be a breach of confidence."
Although his exterior remained calm Peter thought he saw Brown's face tighten slightly in an attempt to contain his anger.

Pleased to have the upper hand Peter continued "I would also like to point out that you have not actually arrested or charged my client with anything else. Any attempt to search his home without my presence or at any time other than at my client's convenience will result in legal action that you can certainly do without."

Peter knew the Police and Criminal Act rules for entry and search of a premises better than he had ever known the Lord's Prayer. For a criminal lawyer it was the Lord's Prayer. Brown had intended to go to the judge's house to question him in the hope that he could get some form of confession. He could then have arrested him without a warrant. As soon as he had done this he could have searched the house provided he was looking for evidence related to the specific offence. A murder weapon would be just such an item; and any judge would forgive any procedural error of one was discovered at the home of the arrested party.

The judge's heart attack and Peter's presence at the house had changed his plan completely. He knew it and Brown knew it. Brown had lost the element of surprise that was often so crucial in any criminal investigation. All they could do was wait until the judge was able to speak to them. Peter decided not to tell them that he had keys to the house. If he thought that the keys were with someone else it would hinder him further.

"You know very well that we would not do that," Brown replied. If he knew that Peter had the keys he did not make it apparent.
"At the very least you will allow me to put an officer on duty, just in case anyone tries to get to him. It would be as much for his protection as anything else."

Or in case the judge decided to discharge himself suddenly, Peter thought to himself. Peter was not enamoured with this idea but he had little choice.

He wished the judge would allow him to divulge the existence of the blackmailer. This would go some way to persuading him of the judge's innocence, but Peter's hands were tied. He could not violate his instructions even if this meant that Brown's suspicions were further aroused.

"I don't think we can achieve much more here tonight," Peter commented.

"Might I suggest that we meet here tomorrow morning at about midday, so that I can have a full conference with his Honour, if he is able, and then we can discuss the matter further. I will call you from my office in the morning to confirm the arrangement."

Brown reluctantly agreed to abide by Peter's conditions and posted an officer outside the judge's room.

As Peter left the hospital his head was buzzing. This was when he was at his best. Under pressure and with little or no time to act. He had to formulate a plan of action to ensure that everything ran smoothly. The first thing he was determined to do was find Charles Napier.

He did not have a clue where to start his search, the only thing he knew so far was that the police couldn't track him down either. As far as Peter was concerned this was not an entirely bad thing, after all he would like to talk to him before DCI Brown got a chance. He had no concrete facts to go on, only an intuition, a feeling. Over the years he had grown to trust these gut reactions. This was what made him an exceptional lawyer and he knew it. It was seven o' clock by the time he left the hospital and adrenaline was coursing through his veins. Catching a taxi he decided to go straight home, he would get into the office for an early start the next day.

He wanted desperately to talk to Naomi. It seemed like an eternity since they had spoken in the morning. She was often his sounding board, with her practical no-nonsense approach, she would be able to direct him precisely to his next move.

He also wanted to celebrate. This was after all the biggest case he had ever tackled. He felt infinitely sorry for the judge but he knew that if he handled this the right way he would be made for life. He could say goodbye to Martin Mather & Co. Naomi would tell him that his anxiety that he was not up to handling the case was unfounded. She would massage and soothe his ego and prepare him for what lay ahead. He needed her now more than ever.

TWENTY-TWO

It was not startling that the flat was immersed in the pitch black of night when Peter arrived home. Theirs was not a nine-to-five existence and there was no blueprint, no routine, to their living together. Either of them could be home first on any day, today it seemed it was his turn.

Peter was mildly surprised when he noticed there was no flashing light on the answer phone, they tended to phone each other if they knew that they were going to be late. They never left a startling or particularly emotional message, just a bold statement of fact. Neither of them were particularly big on expressing their emotions openly. The fact that they phoned each other at all was significant enough. They knew how they felt about each other without having to voice it.

Having said that, if her day had been anything like his, she would not have been able to make it to the phone let alone leave a message. Still he was bothered, it was almost a ritual to leave the message unless they were rowing and he could think of nothing he had done the previous evening which could possibly have upset her.

It needled him that she had not left a message in the way that it always does when a couple who have grown fond of each other expect each other's undivided attention. He was not a man prone to fits of jealousy, but he could not help but yield to a pang of envy that she might be out with another man. She had never made a secret of her past. She had lived a full life, that was the way that she liked to describe it. And he had been a little shocked by the number of partners she had. Then again, as she always argued, if a man had said it, no one would have thought a thing. He had slept with more partners than she had, yet he was still shocked by her past.

He knew that she was right when she said that he had nothing to be jealous of. A relationship was about trust, if two people could not trust each other then there was no point. He was also aware of just how many male admirers waited in the wings to tempt her away.

Moving through the flat he switched on lamps, the way that she liked it. He loved the flat almost as much as she did. His favourite room if you could call it that, it was no more than a corridor, was the kitchen. With its chic handmade wooden units dragged in lime green paint, the Italian stone floor tiles and modern cooking range it emanated a certain warmth, a homeliness. It was ironic that such a kitchen was rarely utilised. Neither of them liked cooking. The surfaces more often than not ended up littered with the silver and plastic trays or foils of various convenience foods. Tonight was no exception. The remnants of Naomi's curry takeaway from the night before sat alone near the sink, the air hinting at her choice.

The faint enticing odour made Peter realise that he was hungry. He had not eaten since lunch. Food often became an irrelevance when he was immersed in something, it was not so much that he forgot to eat, more that he did not have the time. Other things always seemed more important. More out of hope than actual knowledge he opened the door of the fridge. He knew that they had not been shopping for weeks and did not expect to find much in the way of sustenance.

He was not disappointed. The same Marks & Spencer salad, linguini and mushroom sauce that had been there for a fair time sat, forlorn, alone in the fridge. There was however a loaf of bread and a pint of milk, more contemporary additions that seemed recent. Deciding not to risk potential food poisoning he closed the fridge. He would wait until Naomi came home and they would order a pizza.

In one area of domestic services he knew that he would not be disappointed. Grabbing a glass from the Welsh dresser and a bottle opener from the cutlery drawer he moved back into the hall. A pine bottle rack contained twelve bottles of their favourite wine. Alcohol was something that they never stinted on and they made sure that it was constantly stocked. Grabbing a bottle of Chateau Neuf de Pape he moved into the sitting room. Shedding his jacket, throwing it on a chair, he deftly opened the bottle and poured himself a generous glass and sat silently on the large comfortable couch, glass in hand.
He did not want any noise, no television, no music. He wanted to think. Sipping the wine he realised just how tense he was. His neck was taut and knotted as he rolled his head from one side to the other.

The phone shattered his concentration. He was tempted not to answer it at all until it occurred to him that it might be Naomi. Forcing himself out of the succour of the sofa, glass still in hand, he

walked to the phone on a small table in the hall.
"Yes. Peter Ritchie."

He wanted to sound unfriendly in case it was
something to do with work.

A small voice that he almost did not recognise
spoke up after a brief silence. He at once regretted
his stern voice.

"Hello, Daddy," she said.

It was Abigail. Peter's eyes strayed to a picture by
the phone, a picture of his beautiful daughter,
Abigail.

The picture was taken just before her eleventh
birthday. A pretty, dark-haired girl smiling
happily at the camera without a care in the world.
She looked like her mother, with long brown hair,
brown eyes and subtly beautiful features. Peter
sighed, since he split up with Fiona she had
controlled his access with a fist of iron.

Fiona and he were now on amicable terms after
several years of her complaining he was an
irresponsible father whose domestic arrangements
were less than satisfactory. She could not resist
snide references to his relationship with Naomi.
The marriage did not work but he could never
regret Abigail's birth. He only agreed to marry her
because she was pregnant and because he
believed it was the right thing to do. He was not
the marrying type and could not give up his
freedom. Eventually he could take no more and
decided to face up to Fiona rather than carry on
living a lie. Their conversation when he had
broken it to her was as vivid as if it had been
yesterday.

"We got married for all the wrong reasons. I am

only trying to be honest with you."
"You mean you got married for all the wrong reasons. Not me. And how can you call our beautiful child the wrong reasons?" Fiona had retorted. She could not resist twisting the knife; it had been difficult enough for him as it was.
"Don't twist my words. You know I love Abigail. It's us that's the problem," he reasoned. No matter how tempted he was to get angry he wanted a congenial solution. His daughter was too important to him.
"Us. You mean it's you that's the problem. I've given one hundred per cent to this marriage." She could be infuriating at times.
Finally frustrated with the negotiations, he had declared that he was leaving her.

He had told her she could have everything, he didn't want a penny, only to reach an agreement over access to Abigail. He would not let his daughter be dragged through the divorce courts. Fiona retorted sarcastically that he was very generous especially as her father had paid for all that they had. She could not resist hitting upon that raw nerve. He had never wanted anything from her parents. They had insisted on buying them the house. They had their social position to think about.

She had gone on "And as for access, if you walk out on me you'll never see Abigail again. My father will tie you up in litigation for years," she continued.
Peter had begged her "Fiona, please can we try and be civilised about this?" He was not going to give up yet.
"Civilised?" she had screamed. "What are my

parents going to say about this?"

"Very little I should think Fiona. They've hated me from the moment they set eyes on me. I was never good enough for their precious daughter."

In the end he had simply packed his things and gone to stay with an old college friend in London. Fiona Morris Nee Shaw had been his long-time girlfriend. They had been going out on and off since he was thirteen. He had only started going out with her because his raging hormones demanded release. Her parents lived near his in Tamworth. Her father was a highly successful barrister who could afford to accommodate his family in a leafy middle-class neighbourhood of large detached houses. Peter's father was a bank manager and they lived in a more modest semi-detached house. Even then she was a brash, loud, dominant girl, used to getting her way. He had not liked her much, but she had been, still was in fact, beautiful, with her long dark hair and svelte pubescent figure that had begun to lean towards that of a woman.

He pursued her with all the tact of a clumsy teenager on heat throughout a party and when the inevitable moment came he kissed her. From that first, wet, unsophisticated, electrifying kiss he was determined to obtain his first tentative sexual experience. He was not so much in love as in lust. They began to go out with each other from that day on. He would have to wait for some time before he obtained his prize as Fiona was from a good Catholic family. When finally he enticed her to sleep with him it was a messy, clumsy, teenage affair that had left him wondering what all the fuss was about. Only after many practice sessions would he come to enjoy the pleasures of the flesh fully.

He had kept going out with Fiona mainly to keep his parents happy and because his flaming hormones needed some bodily release. It was only when he got to Kingston Polytechnic at the age of eighteen that he found a new source. He discovered his fellow freshers and although he continued to go out with Fiona he embarked on a series of drunken one-night stands and flings. He had discovered the font of freely available sex that he had always dreamed about. Peter was nothing if not honest with Fiona. He told her all about his experiences, stating that they were not really going out together but if she wanted to see him during his holidays that was okay with him. He was fond of her but not in love with her. This arrangement was mutually satisfying for them both until she fell pregnant in 1984.

It seemed ironic to him that the best thing that came out of his marriage, and that which had sounded a resounding death knell for that marriage had been one and the same thing, Abigail.

Abigail, he had not spoken to her for some time. He was surprised at how her voice had changed since the last time. She was his little girl and he found it difficult that she was at the threshold of womanhood. At almost twelve years old she was not the little girl that used to cling to him desperately every time he had to take her to her mother's house. She was already becoming confident, self-assured, she liked to ask awkward questions without being fobbed off with lies.

Questions like "Are you going to marry, Naomi?", "Why did you leave mummy, she says it's because you were messing around?", had become a normality and he always struggled to answer them without undermining his former wife. He did not know why he bothered defending her since she took every opportunity to weaken him as Abigail's father.

"Hello, Beaker, how's tricks?"
Beaker was his pet name for her, derived from squeaker, something he had called her from birth.
"Dad, don't call me that, I've told you that before," she said sternly but laughed despite herself.
"I'm all right," she continued.
"How's your mother?"
He always asked this out of some need to create a semblance of normality for Abigail rather than any feelings for his ex-wife.

Fiona had continued to be hostile to him from the day they had separated. Acting irrationally at every opportunity by withdrawing access, accusing him of turning their daughter against her, or throwing spurious and illegitimate allegations at his feet. It did not help that she had never remarried or formed any significant dependence to another man. He had hoped that she would eventually but over the years he had come to realise that this was not going to happen. She was determined to make him suffer for the rest of his life. Abigail did hint that 'Uncles' Richard, Ian or Michael had dated Fiona for a while but none of them had lasted for very long.

Fiona had recently inherited her father's estate, who had died of cancer. A substantial sum by all accounts and she was paranoid that they were only after her money. The money itself rankled Peter, not because he wanted any of it, the price would be too high for accepting his ex-wife's generosity, but because she still insisted on his paying of maintenance and child support. It had nothing to do with money, the courts had reduced it to a paltry sum, it was her hold on him. She took great pleasure in issuing proceedings through her solicitor if payments were overdue.

Things had taken a turn for the worse when he had moved in with Naomi. Fiona believing that she still had some hold over him had declared open hostility for Naomi, who had the grace to accept the situation with magnanimity. She was not looking to be Abigail's surrogate mother. She accepted that if Peter was to have access Abigail was going to have to stay with them on her weekend visits. She was not in competition with Fiona, despite what she thought, and she always went out of her way to make Abigail's stay fun and interesting.

This in its own way made things worse because they became friends, Naomi was like a big sister to her. They laughed, they joked together, they shopped together and Abigail really looked forward to her stays with them.

Peter could not thank Naomi enough for the way she had handled the situation. She did not prejudge him, she had no preconceived ideas about what her role was. She only became annoyed when she thought of the astringency that was pent up within Fiona and worried what effect it would have on Abigail.

A new round of hostility had begun recently so he was somewhat surprised to hear from her.

"She's okay, you know how it is," Abigail replied anxiously.

"Actually," she continued. "She doesn't know that I'm using the phone."

This was the latest phase of the game, banning Abigail from calling him or Naomi unless she was in the room. He had not even bothered to protest, he knew that it would only aggravate the situation.

"So I can't use the phone for long. You know what she's like, she'll call you a bastard."

"Don't swear, Beaker, I've told you ladies don't swear."

He tried to sound stern but failed. He was like all fathers, putty in her hands. She knew exactly what buttons to press.

She laughed again, the infectious laugh of a soon to be teenager, still full of wide-eyed innocence, still full of hope.

"Dad, you and Naomi swear like troopers, so does Mummy."

She laughed again.

He could not help laughing with her. Whenever he spoke to her he realised how much he missed her. His guilt at not being there for her when she grew up had become a crippling burden to his conscience.

"Anyway, Daddy, the reason I called."

She assumed a cute, businesslike air. A smile spread across his face. He had to put a hand over his mouth to stop laughter bubbling up from his chest. She would not like that.

"I wanted to talk to Naomi. To thank her for the clothes she sent me through the post. They're lovely, everyone at school is jealous of me. They're boss. Is she there?"

Peter did not even know that she had sent a parcel to Abigail. Naomi had not mentioned it, then she would not. It was the little touches that showed how much she cared, but no doubt she would say that she saw the clothes, thought they would look nice on Abigail, and bought them. No ulterior motive, no hidden agenda. Simple as that. Though he doubted Fiona would agree.

"No I'm afraid she's not back from work yet. I'll tell her you called and get her to call you tomorrow."
"Oh." She sounded disappointed.
"Anyway what the hell does *boss* mean?"
He was out of touch with the younger generation and had no idea what this meant. In his day cool and groovy were the buzz words.

She laughed again, her setback forgotten. In her childlike innocence she considered anyone over eighteen ancient.
"It means trendy." She spoke to him as if he was the child.
"I also rang to tell you, remind you, that it's my birthday next Tuesday."
"As if I could forget."

In fact he had forgotten, with everything that had happened her birthday was the last thing on his mind, and he felt immediately contrite. Which is probably exactly what she had intended.

"What do you want?"
He continued aware, within the framework of his guilt, that whatever she demanded he could

202

hardly refuse. He was in her power.

"Well you know that Megadrive you and Naomi got for me last Christmas?"

It was a leading question, whatever she wanted it was obviously expensive.

"Yes," he said. Waiting for the sting.

"I want a couple of new games, but if you just give me the money I'll get them."

That was her way of saying that he was not too good at choosing presents.

"Okay, Beaker, I'll send you the money."

"Thanks, Dad," she said with genuine pleasure.

"How are Grandma and Grandpa," he asked. "Do you still go to their's for tea on Thursdays?"

"Yep. Gran doesn't stop talking about you these days, she says you don't see them nearly enough these days."

He knew that this was his mother's way of having a snipe at Naomi. They got on quite well when they met but his mother could not accept that anyone could replace Fiona. They could not fathom how anyone could leave her. To them she was the perfect wife, the perfect mother. And they had never asked him his side of the story, which hurt him more deeply than he cared to admit.

"I said you and Naomi were busy people, but that you would both come to my birthday party," she continued.

"Give my love to both of them. Where is the party being held?"

"At Granny's, oh say you'll both come Daddy, it's next Saturday. I asked for it to be then, you're not working."

How could he refuse, especially as it was being

held on neutral territory. He did not fancy having to face Fiona, but he knew that everyone would make an effort to keep the peace for Abigail's sake.

"I should think so, I'll talk it through with Naomi and let you know, okay?"
He knew that Naomi would refuse for diplomacy's sake. One ex-wife was enough to contend with. To take Naomi, his scarlet woman, would be a recipe for disaster and they were not too sensitive to ruin it for Abigail. Fiona would find a way to do that anyway and they did not want to be responsible for providing a convenient catalyst.

"Great. I'd better go," she continued.
"And I'll see you next Saturday."
"We're both looking forward to it already. Take care, Beaker, make sure the bed bugs don't bite." She groaned down the phone at this pre-bedtime ritual.
"I love you, Daddy."

The line went dead. He did not like lying to her. It would disappoint her if she knew straightaway that Naomi could not make the party. It was better to tell her nearer the day. Returning to the sofa, wine glass in hand, he flopped himself down onto the soft cushions swinging his legs over one end. He still had his shoes on. His feet had begun to ache. Whenever he was under pressure his feet swelled up and his neck developed a tightness. Naomi had become an expert at massaging the tension away with the help of a bottle of body oil.

Using one of his shoes as a lever he kicked off both without undoing the laces and let them fall to the floor with a dull thump. Downing the glass of wine and pouring himself another he realised that his conversation with Abigail had been just the tonic he needed. He had completely forgotten about the judge, Bobby Black, Charles Napier's whereabouts, everything. Drifting off into thought he almost jumped out of his skin when the phone began to ring shrilly again. This time he was sure it would be Naomi. Maybe it was the hospital telling him that the judge had died and momentarily he saw his bright new career away from Martin Mather & Co evaporate before his eyes. That was a prospect he did not want to contemplate.

When he picked up the phone he was greeted with an eerie silence, only white noise for company.
"Is anyone there?" he asked guardedly in case it was a deep breather. He heard a mechanical click at the other end of the line after what seemed like forever.
"Is anyone there?" he repeated again. The flat mechanical voice that spoke sent a chill to the very heart of his being. It was a voice that he had heard once already that day.
"Good evening, Mr Ritchie. I hope that I have not disturbed you, but I have something rather important to discuss with you. It just could not wait until morning."

Peter thought that the voice contained a hint of amusement, although that was impossible. It was sexless, characterless, making it all the more menacing. He knew at once what the judge must have felt. What could the blackmailer want with him? He did not know what to say, did not know anything that he could say. All he could do was listen.

"We have a mutual friend to discuss so I'll try to keep it brief," the voice rasped quietly.
The judge, he wants to discuss the judge, Peter thought. This could be the break he was looking for. If he could get the blackmailer to divulge something, anything.
On impulse his hand went to his side where the pocket of his jacket would be. The pocket that held the tape. Looking over his shoulder he could just see the jacket thrown untidily over a chair in the living room. He could not believe his luck.

"I take it the mutual friend you are referring to is his Honour Sir Justin Hodge?"
He talked firmly, adopting his best courtroom voice.
"In a manner of speaking, yes," the voice continued.
"I warned the judge not to involve anyone in this matter, a very private matter. I knew that his arrogance would not allow him to do that. I was astonished that he involved you. If only he had not survived the heart attack. Things would be very different. By involving you he has forced me to take further action, to adjust my plan slightly."

He knew exactly what had happened then Peter thought. He must have been watching the judge's house the whole time. This thought made him fee very uncomfortable. If he knew that Peter had been at the judge's house, he must have followed him to the hospital, followed him home. He might be watching the flat right now. The hospital had been full of people, any one of them could have been the blackmailer.

"What do you want? If you know as much as you claim, you will know that the police are already fully aware of what you are up to. I even have a recording of you threatening the judge."

The mechanical voice rattled in a sick parody of a human laugh.

"Mr Ritchie, please do not insult my intelligence. We are too clever for that. I know that you have told the police nothing. If we cannot be completely honest with each other than I will hang up. You will have to find out my next move in your own time. What is it to be, Mr Ritchie?"

"Okay, okay, play it your way", Peter said with too much desperation in his voice. He wished that he could hide his obvious human emotions behind a machine.

"I am glad that we understand each other, Mr Ritchie," the machine droned.

Peter was beginning to feel irritated by the politeness of the mystery caller.

"I have no quarrel with you, Mr Ritchie, as I said it is unfortunate that his Honour chose to involve you. I admit I found it an odd choice, you were hardly bosom buddies before this whole affair began."

He has certainly done his research Peter thought. This struck him as odd. Why would he need to know all about him?

"You are a very lucky man, Mr Ritchie, a very lucky man indeed."

"What do you mean?" Peter blurted without thinking.

"You have a beautiful home, a beautiful daughter,

a beautiful woman, and a successful career. Many men would count themselves as fortunate to have one of those things. You have all four." He paused.

"Listen you fucking arsehole, if you touch Naomi or my daughter I'll fucking kill you. Stop playing games with me and get to the fucking point."

The voice laughed again. A laugh that pierced Peter's soul with its inhumanity.

"In particular I admire your girlfriend, such a wonderfully spirited woman. She put in an impeccable performance in Guildford today. You should have seen her. It was inspirational. Truly inspirational."

Peter hoped that the man was playing with him, making his point. Nothing had happened to her, she was out drinking with a friend. She would fall in the door in a drunken stupor any moment, tottering on her heels with her teeth stained red by the wine she had guzzled. Even as he thought it, the horrible truth was beginning to dawn on him.

"You bastard, if you have harmed her in any way at all I'll track you down. I'll rip you apart with my bare hands."

Peter was losing control of himself. He was playing into this man's hands but he did not care, he was scared and frightened. Instinct had taken over from reason.

"I'm glad you feel that way, Mr Ritchie. I would hate to have to hurt her. It will not come to that if you do as you are told."

Peter knew that he was defeated. In that moment he knew exactly what the judge must have felt. He was adrift, out of control and at the mercy of whoever this man was.

"What do you want?" Peter responded in a desolate whisper.

"Nothing really. Just make sure the judge is prosecuted and found guilty of the murder. It will not be the first time that an innocent man has been found guilty of something he did not do. And remember I'll be watching you."

"What about Naomi?" Peter cried.

The blackmailer had hung up. He was shouting at the dialling tone.

Dropping the phone to the floor, he stared at the picture that hung on the wall above the phone table. They had bought it together on holiday in Thailand. It had cost them fifty pence in a local market. Naomi had insisted on haggling over the price even though it was cheap.

Peter did not know what to do. He no longer felt hungry, he no longer felt tired. His feet no longer ached, his neck was no longer knotted. He felt numb. He felt nothing. The walls of the room pressed in on him and dropped away. He no longer knew who he was. His home, his job, nothing meant anything anymore.

Peter had not slept at all by the time the milkman called at the flat the next morning. The clinking of bottles and the milkman's happy tuneless whistle made him look at his watch. It was seven-thirty. He had not moved from the sofa all night. He was still dressed in the same clothes. He had drunk the bottle of wine although he could not actually remember drinking anything. He had not been drunk, he knew that. His nervous system was too keyed up to allow the effects of the alcohol to work on him. Despite the lack of sleep he felt wide awake. He knew what he had to do. The cold light of morning told him that he had not imagined it. That it was real.

He had to behave as normal. Naomi's life depended on it. Behaving normally meant going to work as usual. Pulling himself up from the sofa he headed for the shower. In a daze he performed his daily ritual with detachment.

Allowing the water to course over his body he turned his face to the powerful jet of water. Peter realised that whoever he was he did not know him that well, he merely wanted to give that impression. If he did he would have had to carry out extensive surveillance of his life and how could he have done that? He himself had said he was surprised that the judge had involved him.

If he did he would know that by forcing Peter's hand he was playing a very dangerous game. He had always had a strong contempt for people in power who abused their position. His whole life had been devoted to the fight of the underdog. Now that he was the underdog he was more determined than ever to win.

During his long night he had decided that he would go along with the blackmailer superficially. He knew that to find him he would have to tread extremely carefully. No matter how industrious this man was he could not follow his every move, listen to his every phone call.

He knew now more than ever that the secret of

the blackmailer's identity lay in what both the judge and Charles Napier could tell him. Blackmailers were nearly always known to their victims.

Extracting the information from the judge would not be that difficult, he was after all not going anywhere in the physical sense. Charles Napier was however more problematic. He had little or nothing to go on apart from the fact that he knew what he had looked like two years ago. If Charles had disappeared, Peter knew that it was by design rather than accident.

If he could not stop the blackmailer within the boundaries of the law he would do it his own way. He had never been a violent man but under the circumstances his murderous intentions sat comfortably with his deep-seated fervour for justice. They did not feel alien to him. This man had taken the woman he loved.

Finishing his shower he padded into the bedroom, a towel wrapped carelessly around his waist. The silence in the flat was deafening, and he fought the urge to crumple onto the bed in a helpless heap. Naomi needed him now and he had to be strong for both of them. He felt detached from reality as if he was in a scene from a movie.
He had one more task to perform before he headed for the office. He had to explain Naomi's absence from chambers. They would be expecting her this morning. He already had an idea of what he would say. He would say that she had caught the flu that had been doing the rounds, that she would be working from home for the rest of the week at least.

Part of being a good lawyer meant being a good actor, forever concealing your true feelings behind an unreadable poker face. Peter must have succeeded better than he could ever imagine. Even though the journey was conducted in a daze no one had suspected a thing. Rushing to his office in order to avoid any confrontation he was intercepted by Paula. She was surprised to see him. It was only eight am. Twice in two days was unheard of.

She almost scared him to death when she spoke. He had not seen her. He was busy taking off his barber.
"Morning, Peter, early again, them upstairs will have to start paying you a proper wage if you carry on like this."

She was smiling, carrying the obligatory morning post which Peter noticed with relief was extremely light. He laughed, or rather he faked a laugh. It must have been good he thought because Paula laughed with him. She proffered the post to him.
"Morning, Paula. Anything I should know about in this lot?" he continued.
"Peter, I'm only just getting used to the new punctual you, I haven't had a chance to look through it yet."

A look of concern passed over her face.
"Are you all right?" she asked full of concern.
"I'm fine, why?"
"Well you look tired this morning."
Peter sighed inwardly with relief. Considering he had not slept at all he probably did look tired.
"You know what it's like Paula. I had a late night

with Naomi."

It was the first thing that occurred to him. It was amazing how easily he could lie when he put his mind to it. Focusing on Paula's face he tried not to think of Naomi. He could not afford to let anyone know the fear and anger behind his banal façade, it would be playing into the blackmailer's hands.

Paula laughed.
"I'd have thought that was the last thing on your mind, with everything you've got on your plate at the moment. Still, if you've got a secret for all that energy you ought to bottle it and sell it. You'd make a fortune."
Peter moved around behind the desk and sat down in his chair as casually as he could.
"I don't want to take any calls today. All I know is that I'm scheduled for a meeting sometime this morning. That and other related matters are likely to take up most of the day. The next few days actually. Anything going on here that I should know about?"
"Well it's funny you should ask. I don't know what it is you're working on at the moment but whatever it is it's stirring up the hornets."
"What do you mean?" Peter asked casually, wondering what she could know.
"After you left yesterday afternoon things went mad. The Colonel was looking for you all afternoon. Mrs Dailey said that he received a phone call in the afternoon. He would not tell her what it was about but it doesn't take Einstein to work it out with him looking for you. As if that was not enough he called a full emergency partners meeting when one wasn't scheduled for two weeks."

Peter knew that partners meetings were called at the end of every month. He had never heard of one being called at such short notice.

"What's more it went on for more than two and a half hours. Mrs Dailey wasn't allowed to take the minutes and she says they all left with very serious looks on their faces."

The meetings never lasted more than ten minutes unless something really important had to be discussed.
"Is he in the building?" Peter asked knowing that he would be. He would have to avoid any confrontation with him, as he did not rust his temper.
"That's what's even odder, he's been here since seven. He usually plays golf today," Paula replied.
"Has he asked for me yet?"
"No. He's been in a meeting with Hale since he got in."

At least he had some time before Mather confronted him.
"Do me a favour Paula, if he or Mrs Dailey ask for me tell him I'm not in yet. It's not entirely true as you can see but, since I'll be leaving for my meeting as soon as possible it's not a complete lie."

As an afterthought he added something else. "Whatever you do, don't let Mather see the Black files. Tell him you don't know where they are, anything." He sensed somehow the files were important.

"Say no more Peter, lying is part of the job description. What's this all about?"

"I wish I could tell you Paula, but I can't."

He really meant that. He wished that he could tell her everything. She turned to leave the room.

"As soon as you can will you get me DCI Brown at Holborn."

"Okay."

And with that she left his office shutting the door quietly behind her. Picking up the four files from the desk he looked around for somewhere to put them. Somewhere no one would find them. Walking to a corner of the room he buried them under another pile of files. Having a disorganised office had its benefits.

He needed to occupy his mind while he waited for Paula to get hold of DCI Brown. If DCI Brown had spoken to Mather he would soon find out.

Shuffling the papers in front of him the Brixton Prison letter had caught his attention. It was prison issue stationery given to the inmates. He did not know of any of his clients that were serving time at Her Majesty's pleasure. Who could be writing to him? He often received referrals or recommendations from other criminals that he had impressed and his reputation had built up within the hallowed walls of Brixton where more than one of his clients had been incarcerated in the past. Pulling the letter from the pile he examined it closer.

Whoever it was that had written, they had the worst handwriting that he had ever see. It was difficult for him to decipher anything, but concentrating hard he managed to make out most of what it said. It was short and to the point. Prisoners were subject to strict censoring, anything controversial would be blanked out with black pen.

Although he did not have the envelope he knew that it would bare the examination mark of the Governor's department.

The letter itself was unremarkable. It's contents simple

Dear Mr Ritchie,

Please visit me today. A mutual friend recommended you to me. I have information you may consider crucial.

Peter was beginning to lose patience with the author when his eyes rested on the signature. Squinting at it he was not sure if he was imagining it. Pulling the piece of paper nearer to his face he looked closely at it. In scraggly blue biro the name at the bottom of the paper was that of the evasive Charles Napier.

He could not believe Brown had not thought of looking for their star witness within their own data banks.

Picking up the phone he buzzed Paula at her desk.
"Yes," she answered.
"Have you managed to get hold of DCI Brown yet?"
"No. I've tried several times. The lines are busy.

Do you want me to keep trying?"

Peter looked at his watch. It was ten past eight, if he moved quickly he could go to see Charles Napier before going to see the judge.

"Yes. When you get hold of him, tell him I'll call later to arrange a time when we can meet at the hospital. In the meantime I want you to get hold of Brixton to arrange a meeting with one Charles Napier at about nine. I know it's irregular but explain that I've got something very important to discuss with him regarding the case. They know me well, it shouldn't be too difficult if you stress how important it is."

Normally appointments had to be fixed well in advance but he was hoping that they would make an exception for him. They had done so many times in the past. He had to talk to him before anyone else discovered his whereabouts.

"A new client?" Paula asked.

She sounded disgruntled at the amount of work that this would involve.

"You could say that. I know it's a lot to ask, Paula, but I'd be very grateful. This is a priority matter. You can worry about DCI Brown once this is fixed."

Peter was hardly able to contain the excitement he felt. He had to believe that this was the first piece of the jigsaw that would lead him to the identity of the blackmailer.

This story continues in The Judge: Part 2